MICHAEL DECAMP

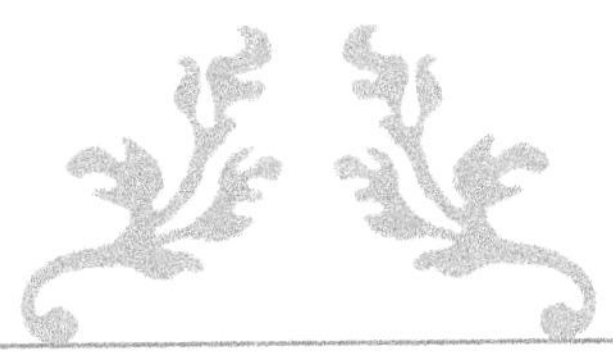

THE PURVEYOR OF DEATH

Doc Moon, Book One

Michael DeCamp

Acknowledgements

As a young person growing up in central Indiana, my late Friday nights were terrorized by Sammy Terry, the zombie host of WTTV-4's weekly monster movies. I want to thank him for scaring me so consistently, but alas, the actor who portrayed him has passed away in real life. I was so enamored by the classic horror movies such as Dracula, The Wolfman, and Frankenstein that when I grew older, I subscribed to the magazine *Famous Monsters of Filmland*. It was almost inevitable, as I began to publish novels, that I would be compelled to write a horror story. This book is that first foray into the genre. I hope you enjoy it.

I am indebted to several individuals who were influential in the completion of this book. I want to take a few moments to recognize them now. I utilized five Beta Readers who gave me invaluable feedback on the earliest version of the story: Jeremy Garrison, Kristina Seifert, Natasha Rodgers, Rosalie King, and Karen E Laine. They helped me fix some obvious errors, identify inconsistencies, and fill in gaps—among other things. My editor, Sherri Stewart, then did the nuts and bolts work of fixing my many grammar, word tense, and phrasing errors—another invaluable resource. (I did a great deal more work on this after her review, so if you find mistakes, blame me, not her.) There is a map of Cutters Notch, Indiana included in this book. I hand-drew it originally, but my friend, Mark Callahan recreated it in his CAD program so that you have a much better (more legible) rendition. I must recognize my publisher, Cynthia Hickey of Winged Publications, for supporting my works and making sure they have a channel to the market. Thank you, one and all.

The undercurrent of classic popular music mentioned throughout this book was an unplanned, happy accident. The works of the various artists I'm about to mention sprang into my mind as I wrote, so I incorporated that inspiration into the prose. Thank you to the late Glen Campbell, to Bob Seger and Willie Nelson, and especially to The Steve Miller Band. If you are unfamiliar with The Steve Miller Band's *The Joker*, go download it and give it a listen.

Lastly, none of this would be possible without my wife, Nancy DeCamp. Her patience, encouragement, and support are what keep my creative spirit alive. If you see her, give her a pat on the back. Thank you, Nancy, for all you do.

Dedication

For my much-loved, miniature Australian shepherd…
Leo
(King Leonidas)
During his sixteenth and last year of life, he began to
get up extra early—between 4 and 5 a.m. every morning.
Since I'd generally be the one to get up with him, I used
that extra time to write. Specifically, I wrote this book.
Thank you, Leo.

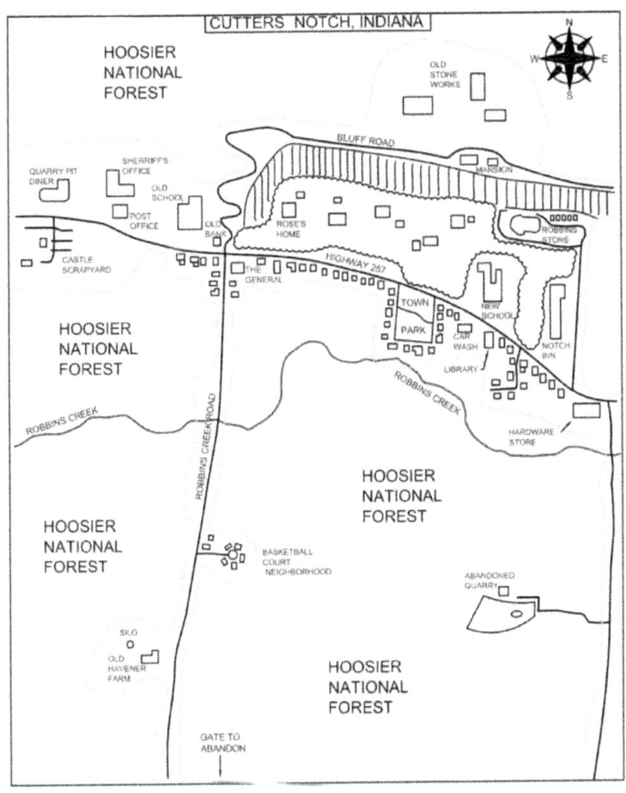

Map courtesy of my friend, Mark Callahan from Indianapolis, Indiana..

Prologue
11:30 p.m., July 22nd
Journal Excerpt

It was midnight last night when I saw my own death. When I say that, I don't mean my life flashed before my eyes in some metaphorical way. It was exactly the opposite. My actual gruesome, bloody death washed across my vision, causing me to stumble and choke as my heart leapt into my throat. I lost my balance, stumbled, and nearly fell in a ditch. You see, I was walking with the moon high over my head and the meager lights of Cutters Notch, Indiana were just up ahead. All at once, strobing scenes of violence filled my vision.

I was outside. Likely here in this park. Trees overhead. Shadows all around. A nearby streetlamp providing just enough light for me to scribble in my notebook. Then it happened. Flashing teeth. Glaring yellow eyes. Tearing skin, snapped tendons, and shredded muscles. There was blood. So much blood.

When I came back to myself, I was on my knees at the edge of the darkened road, shaken. My head was down, and I was breathing too fast, hyperventilating. It took a couple minutes to gather my wits and get back to my feet.

———•●•———

According to the notes in my journal, viewing my violent demise in advance was not a unique experience. Still, it felt like the first time because I couldn't remember the other events. My only choice was to trust my notes. They were the closest thing I had to a long-term memory.

Memories didn't stick in my head if they were generated more than twenty-four hours in the past. I was suffering from a full-blown case of amnesia. Was it the result of some traumatic experience or caused by some other factor? I just didn't know. I could remember information but not experiences. For example, I knew how to do things like read, operate appliances, and defend myself, but I have no idea how I learned to do them. It's like in wiping clean the whiteboard of my mind, the affliction only removed the board, the wall, the room, and the people, leaving seemingly random information printed on nothing. The knowledge is left hanging there in the open space of my brain.

———•●•———

Journal Excerpt

That vision of my death was last night. Whatever those scenes depict will happen to me very soon. According to the pattern in my journal, the events of my potential demise always occur roughly twenty-four hours after the respective vision. The time is nearly up, so here I sit in the dark on a picnic

table at the edge of Cutters Notch Town Park—
awaiting my fate and scribbling in the day's details
as fast as I can.

One
Just after midnight the previous night.

The light of a half-moon splashed a whitewash across the pavement as I walked into town from the west. It was the shortest night of the year—summer solstice. The air was still warm from the heat of the earlier sun, and a light breeze ruffled the long, light brown whiskers on my bearded face. I was tired. I'd been walking since breakfast, following the direction of my instinct, as I continued along the course toward my ultimate destination: Sarasota, Florida. I'm not sure why Sarasota seems to be my destiny, but I was going because both my notebook and my intuition told me that's where I needed to go.

My journal periodically reminds me of where I'm going, but it's my instinct that keeps my feet headed in that direction. I don't know where I started walking. It couldn't have been that long ago because I only have one notebook, and I'm only a quarter of the way into it.

Each day, I get more detailed in my descriptions of the journey. The early postings were slim pickings. That said, maybe I didn't start writing right away. I don't recall for sure. Even with the scant details, there are some crazy stories in these lined pages.

As I walked along in the night air, I could still recall my breakfast. Three eggs, sunny-side up, a lot of bacon, and some fresh hash browns. I skipped the toast and sopped up the eggs with the potatoes. The meal was magnificently prepared by an older woman on a farm somewhere between Cutters Notch and Vincennes, Indiana. The woman was kind enough to feed me after she found me sleeping in her barn. She poked me awake with a Remington 12-gauge, but smiled and asked if I was hungry. As I strolled into the edge of Cutters Notch, I couldn't remember crawling into that woman's barn the previous night. Amnesia removed those details, so it must have been more than twenty-four hours ago.

Tonight, walking in the moonlight, I paused after the terrifying death vision. With my right hand, I pulled the clear plastic water bottle from the side pocket of my cargo pants and took a couple gulps. Then I splashed the rest of it across my face. My hand shook as I held the empty container in the moonlight. It's disconcerting to see your own death, especially if every time it happens, it's as if it's never happened before.

Ahead of me, the lights of the town twinkled. To my left was a diner—closed. The darkened sign said it was the Quarry Pit. "Dig the Food," was added under its name. I chuckled, grateful for the comic relief. Continuing toward Cutters Notch, I noted the dumpster in the back corner of the parking lot. "I'm not that hungry yet," I mumbled. I didn't recall ever dumpster diving, but maybe I just never noted it in the journal.

As I passed a tall chain-link fence on my right, piles of dented and twisted cars loomed over the top of the coiled-wire strands. Strips of plastic blocked some of the junk from view, but gaps and large hinged gates provided a clear line of sight into the scrapyard. I paused, feeling drawn into the mounds of steel, aluminum, plastic, and rubber. It was like an invisible cord was tied to my belt, tugging me toward the maze of discarded vehicular waste.

I walked over and checked the padlock. Secure.

No way in unless I wanted to scale the fence and crawl over the wrapped wire with its barbs or blades, trying to avoid being sliced or cut up. Something was pulling at me, beckoning me, but I resisted. It didn't feel urgent, just insistent. "Maybe I'll come back," I told whatever was calling to me.

There was no traffic. Nothing moved except for the occasional raccoon or skunk. An opossum glared at me from under a shrub, showing its sharp teeth. Streetlights appeared ahead but nothing that indicated any human activity. Maybe I could find someplace to catch some sleep—a soft bed of pine needles was my best hope. I slowed at a large vacant boarded-up school on my left. *Hmm, maybe.* There wouldn't be any running water in the building, and I needed running water. I was thirsty and needed to refill my empty bottle.

I kept moving, strolling past a dilapidated bank building that was giving off an ominous vibe. Then I angled toward the convenience store on the diagonal corner. A sign on a pole read, "The General." Minimal lights. It was obviously closed. I supposed twenty-four-hour convenience wasn't a thing in this part of Indiana. Still, there had to be a faucet for a hose somewhere on the outside of the building.

I found it on the right side. Someone had removed the knob from the valve. No water for me there. "Ugh." My thirst suddenly intensified. By necessity, my solution would be an outdoor spigot on someone's house. Before I went looking though, I gave into my need for food, dove into the dumpster beside the store, and came out with a couple of out-of-date Twinkies packages.

Out on the road again, I passed the first driveway on my left. It led into the trees with a massive cliff face as a backdrop. I couldn't see a house, but it had to be back there. Just then I got another vibe. It said, "You're welcome here. Come on in." Without hearing words, I gleaned those actual phrases inside my mind. They seemed too friendly, maybe a little too eager for me to approach—a trap, perhaps? After all, most of the homes in my twenty-four hours' worth of memory had nothing to say in actual words. Usually, they just gave off feelings—ominous or welcoming or indifferent. I decided to see what the next driveway offered.

The following gravel drive angled across a wooded yard directly to a huge, white house with a massive balcony across the front. Most of the underbrush had been cleared out so I could see accent lighting in the shrubbery along the foundation. With all the detailed landscaping, there was bound to be a live garden hose somewhere close by. However, the sign for the electric dog fence changed my thinking and I kept moving. I liked dogs, but my sense told me they may not like strangers in their yard in the dark.

Across the road, the houses were smaller and closer to the street. Most were two-bedroom bungalows, and most were dark. No dogs in sight. Easier pickings, or so I thought.

Suddenly, my mouth grew unnaturally dry. I spit out a Twinkie when I couldn't generate enough saliva to chew it. I felt a building anxiety and nervous energy welling up inside me. Anticipation of an impending and unknown danger? Goosebumps rose on my arms. Adrenaline surged in my muscles. All my senses sharpened. Suddenly, I noticed new details in the shadows. I could hear mice in the grass. It was weird. I'd read about my previous similar experiences when I'd reviewed my journal earlier in the day, but it gave me no idea how these things hit me. It felt like the first time.

I crossed the road toward a small yellow house with the front windows all brightly lit. The front screen door flew open as I approached and a person slammed backward through it, knocking the door completely around on its hinges. The body landed hard on the wooden porch, then rolled down the three steps to the tiny front yard.

A man followed the body out and loomed over the figure writhing in the grass. Closing the gap, I realized the figure on the ground was a woman. She was curled up in a ball, her hands wrapped around the back of her neck. Whimpering, she rolled to a fetal position, her back to the man.

"Please stop," she moaned.

The couple was so caught up in their violent drama, they didn't notice me walking along the sidewalk. The rattling of an old AC unit camouflaged my footsteps.

A light came on in the house next door. I heard the deadbolt being released even over the AC noise. My accentuated hearing was better than the brute's I was approaching.

"Get your ass back in the house," the man yelled at the woman. He had a beer in his left hand. It slopped out as he leaned over his wife or girlfriend or whatever she was to him. At a minimum, she was his victim. "Get up and get back inside," he added as he grabbed her by her long brown hair. When he jerked her upward, I intervened.

"Let her go," I said loudly but with as much calmness as the adrenaline in my system would allow.

I can't remember if I'm in the habit of stepping into domestic disputes or not. In the moment, I didn't have time to check my journal, but it seemed like the right thing to do, dangerous as it was. Seeing some drunken dude abusing a smaller woman simply didn't sit right with me, and since I'm driven by instinct rather than memory, my instinct said to put a stop to it.

An old man stepped out on his porch at the house

next door. "Come on, Ronnie," the man begged. "Cool down. It's late. Some of us are trying to sleep." The man wore pajama bottoms, a ragged, plain t-shirt, and slippers. His ruffled hair was flattened on one side.

Ronnie, the abuser, stood there with a brew in one hand and the girl's hair in the other. He glared at me but addressed his sleepy neighbor. "Shut up, Pete! Go back inside and mind your business." Then he let go of the girl's hair. At least I'd accomplished that much.

When the young woman on the ground struggled to rise. Ronnie pushed her back down with his foot as he stepped over to confront me. He crumpled his beer can and tossed it in the bushes. It landed on a coiled water hose that I'd never get the chance to use. My mouth felt dryer than ever.

"I'm calling the sheriff," Pete the neighbor said as he stepped back inside.

"You do that, Pete," Ronnie stated. He puffed out his chest inside a stained white muscle shirt; his eyes shot daggers in my direction. "When they get here, they can scrape this guy off the pavement." A moment later, Pete was peering out at us from his front window, phone to his ear.

Ronnie began posturing, perhaps trying to both work up his own courage to fight and, at the same time, intimidate me. I assessed him, this wonder of human maleness. He was shorter than me—less than six feet tall. He had a barrel chest, but his beer gut stuck out a little beyond his pectorals. In his nylon basketball shorts and ankle-length sport socks with no shoes, he presented the twisted image of a male fashion disaster. The guy even sported a tattoo on his left arm—a muscle car doing a wheely across his bicep with oversized front tires.

Ronnie was maybe in his late twenties, used to be an athlete, but in recent years had probably focused more on setting beer-drinking records than winning sports trophies. His eyes bugged out below his prominent forehead and crewcut. His scruffy chin showed a couple of days' worth of growth. My overall assessment—he could likely do some damage if he got a punch in on me, but I sensed I could handle him.

"Are you okay, miss?" I asked, leaning so I could see the girl. She lifted herself up on the palms of her hands, whimpered, and then scooted back toward the small shrubs that lined the porch.

"You don't talk to my girl," Ronnie growled.

"If she's your girl, it seems like a pretty bad way to treat her," I replied.

"Yeah, well, she pissed me off. Now, you'd best get moving 'cause you're the one pissing me off now."

I don't know that I'm a brave man. Then again, I guess I don't know that I'm not. I'd have to check the journal for evidence either way. Still, I couldn't just walk away and leave that young woman to her fate. The porch light illuminated her flushed face, and I could see tears streaking mascara across her cheeks.

"I think maybe I'll stay right here and wait for Pete's sheriff to arrive." My eyes locked hard on his, trying to send the message that I had no fear. Something inside—maybe some prior training I didn't actively recall or maybe a general instinct—told me that guys who beat on their ladies are often bullies with a great deal of personal insecurity. Regardless, I wasn't giving him any ground.

Ronnie, temporarily frozen in place, glared at me. I apparently didn't react the way he expected. After a moment, he stepped into my personal space, raised his shoulders, puffed his chest again, and balled his fists. "I'm gonna give you one more chance to move on down the road." He spat the words out through gritted teeth. "If you aren't gone in about five seconds, I'm gonna pound you into the sidewalk."

I smiled at him, even chuckled a little, as I carefully lowered my backpack to the grass beside the sidewalk. Straightening to my full height, which showed me to be a couple inches taller than my nemesis, I glared right back at him.

Now, as I jot this down and have had some time to think it over, maybe that wasn't the best idea. I mean, it certainly wasn't designed to diffuse the situation. Still, it had the desired effect. I saw doubt flare across his pupils. He'd hoped to intimidate me, but my response gave him pause. He didn't know me, after all, and he didn't know my capabilities. In that moment, neither did I. All I knew was that he didn't scare me, and I could almost feel each of his thoughts as they raced across his brain. Anger. Fear. Doubt. Hesitation. Embarrassment. Hurt. More anger.

Over Ronnie's shoulder, I could see that the girl was starting to get a grip. She stood and wrapped her arms in a self-hug. She was shivering, though it was close to eighty degrees even just after midnight. The moon cast dark shadows under her eyes. Then again, that could have been the smeared mascara.

"Get moving," Ronnie demanded, pointing east.

"Maybe you should go," I offered. "If the sheriff is on his way, you're the only one who's actually assaulted anyone." I continued to smile. "After all, I'm just taking a stroll on a public sidewalk," I added with a shrug.

The abuser tried to shove me, but I'd set my feet and didn't move. He tried again, harder. This time, I backed off and twisted, timing my move with his, and using his momentum against him, I caused him to stumble forward. Tripping over my feet, he landed and rolled over. As a result, we'd reversed positions, putting his lady behind me. I realized that wasn't a particularly safe position, so I moved to the side a couple paces to keep them both in my field of vision.

Ronnie scrambled to his feet. Over his shoulder, I could see flashing blue lights approaching from the direction of that little general store. Earlier I'd passed the sheriff's office, positioned as it was behind the local post office. I knew it was a short drive. "Here they come," I announced.

As the car pulled up next to us, Ronnie growled through gritted teeth. "You watch yourself. You're gonna pay."

I smiled again, but my grin quickly faded. In that moment, I felt the monster's eyes on me for the first time. I didn't yet know who or what it was, only that it was watching. My eyes darted from tree to tree across the road and saw nothing. It was an unsettling feeling— like a thousand little pairs of ant legs creeping up my spine. The short hairs on the back of my neck stood up and took notice. I felt a chill down deep in my soul.

The deputy exited his cruiser, placed his hat on his head, and joined us on the sidewalk. The nameplate on his chest said his name was Randall. "Ronnie, you back off now," he instructed.

"Gator, me and Joanie was sittin' on the porch, minding our own business, when this dude started insulting her." The man was an abuser and a liar, too, but I expected as much. "I had to defend her," Ronnie added, as if he were some kind of hero.

"Here we go," I mumbled. They were calling one another by first names, although I'd never thought of *Gator* as a first name before. Small-town Indiana. I should've figured they'd know one another. Whether that was good or bad depended on how much integrity Deputy Gator Randall had as an officer of the law.

Deputy Randall sized me up. He obviously knew Ronnie, but he didn't know me. "Who are you, and what are you doing here in the middle of the night?" he asked me. "Are you visiting someone, or are you just drifting through?"

In that moment, my amnesia became problematic. I knew I wasn't visiting anyone, but who I was…well, that was a tougher question. It'd been over twenty-four hours since I'd looked at that portion of my journal. I couldn't remember my own name. Ignoring the first part of his question, I responded to the second half. "I'm passing through town. I was walking down the street when I saw that young woman come tumbling out the door. She rolled backwards down the steps and then curled up in a ball. As I crossed over to check on her, this Ronnie fellow followed her out. He grabbed her by the hair, and I told him to stop."

"Mm, hmm," Gator mumbled. He stared hard at Ronnie. His face was an unreadable tablet of stone.

The neighbor stepped back out onto his porch as I spoke, still wearing his pajama bottoms and slippers. His gray hair continued to show signs of bed head. The deputy turned to him. "What'd you see, Pete?"

"Me? I didn't see or hear anything 'cept these two facing off." He pointed at me and Ronnie.

Ronnie grinned back at me. He had his neighbor cowed. He knew it and now I knew it. If the deputy didn't believe me, there was no one to back me up.

Deputy Randall turned his eyes toward the young woman. "Joanie, are you okay? Was Ronnie hurting you?"

Joanie shook her head. She was still hugging herself and shaking like it was forty degrees outside, despite the warm summer breeze. "No sir. It's like Ronnie said. We were minding our own business on the porch when this guy started the trouble." She tried hard to look sincere, but the streaks of mascara across her cheekbones told another story. I only hoped the deputy could read it.

Leave it to me to walk into town at midnight, and the first person I meet is the town bully. Seems Ronnie got his way through intimidation. Even the girl wasn't going to back me up. It would all come down to how well Gator knew the guy.

Pete shook his head when Joanie spoke, then stepped back inside his house. Never mind that he didn't have the guts to tell the truth either. Instead, he seemed to look down his nose at the real victim when she was too scared to tell it, too. Being judgmental doesn't require personal integrity, it seems.

The deputy quietly assessed the situation, looking first at Ronnie, then at Joanie, finally back at me. "You didn't give me your name."

"I don't remember it." At least my integrity was intact.

"You don't remember your own name?"

"Not at the moment," I replied with some hesitation, trying to come off as sincere. "Sorry. I really don't. It's an amnesia thing."

"Hmm." After contemplating that for a few moments as he studied my face, he asked to see some identification. "You do have an ID, right?"

I didn't remember the answer to that question either, so I started searching my pockets for a wallet. I found a Twinkie wrapper, a comb, an ink pen, and my plastic water bottle, but no wallet. "It appears I don't have an ID on me. I'm sorry."

Turning back to the domestically-challenged couple, Deputy Randall pointed toward the door. "Ronnie, you and Joanie get in the house, and don't let me get wind of any more trouble from you tonight. You understand?"

"Yessir," they replied in stereo.

Ronnie smirked at me, then turned away. Joanie

wrapped her arm around his waist, and he trundled her inside before closing the front door. Now, it was just me and Deputy Gator Randall. At least Ronnie wasn't beating on the girl anymore. I'd met my primary goal.

"So, you don't know your own name, and you don't have an ID. Is that right?"

"Seems that way. I'm sorry." And I really was. By not minding my own business, I'd made my way into trouble with the local law and would likely get no credit for saving Joanie's skin. On the bright side, I could end up with a bed in an air-conditioned building, even if there were bars on the door.

"Maybe you have some ID in that backpack." He pointed at the camouflaged bag sitting on the grass nearby. I'd forgotten about that, too. It wasn't the amnesia; it was all the excitement. "Gather it up and look inside, but be slow about it. I don't need any surprises. You don't have any weapons, do you?"

"Nope. No weapons, sir." At least I was pretty sure that was true. I held the bag up, testing its weight. Not much inside. I sure didn't remember seeing any ID in there, but I checked the pockets anyway. I found only a ten-dollar bill and a pack of gum. The woman who'd fixed my breakfast had given me that money, too. Inside the main zippered compartment, I found my journal. No ID card, though. And luckily, no weapons.

"Okay. Tell you what," Deputy Randall said, "drop the bag, then turn around and face my cruiser."

"Are you arresting me?"

"Nope, but you're not getting in my car unless I check you over first."

"I'm getting in your car?" Maybe I'd get to enjoy an air-conditioned sleep space after all.

"You are, son. I take in lost puppies and drifters. My wife says I have 'sucker' printed on my forehead. I saw you wander into town a little while ago and was already thinking about tracking you down to see if you needed some help. Pete's call gave me just the extra excuse I needed to get off my butt and do it."

I leaned on his car, face first, hands spread.

"Anything in your pockets? Anything that'll poke or stick me?"

"Beats me, but I don't think so."

He checked. Nothing there. After turning me back to face him, he opened the rear door like a chauffeur and offered me a seat. I grabbed my bag and hopped in willingly. After all, it was cooler inside.

As Deputy Randall turned around in Ronnie's driveway, I saw the woman-beater watching me through his front window. At least I seemed to have gotten his mind off hurting Joanie. Now, it seemed, he just wanted to hurt me.

"You got some place to sleep tonight?" The deputy's eyes peered at me through his rearview mirror. They looked friendly.

"I don't think so," I said. "I guess I was hoping for a soft bed of pine needles under a tree somewhere."

"I thought not."

He didn't say anything more, returning his eyes to the road. I rested my head back and felt the rumble of the tires on the pavement as we covered the short drive to the jail. The big old house on the right, across from the little store, once again sent out its vibes for me to visit, and the junkyard sent me vibes to come help. I simply closed my eyes and let it all soak in. What else was hidden below the surface of this little nowhere town?

The deputy steered the car to the rear of the municipal building, a squat structure built with limestone blocks behind the post office. Then he pulled into a reserved spot near a door. "Authorized Personnel Only" was stenciled on the glass. After releasing me from the rear seat, he stepped back so I could get out.

"Thank you, sir," I said.

"No problem."

I took a deep breath. Something felt weird. Ominous. Taking another look at the deputy, I could see nothing in him but a friendly, yet cautious curiosity. The odd feeling was coming from something else. Slowly, I turned in a circle, my eyes scanning the edge of the forest that wrapped around the parking lot. Someone or something was watching me. A slight breeze fluttered my hair even as goosepimples rose on my arms. There was something nearby. Something bad.

"Come on," Randall said. "Let's go inside."

"Absolutely," I replied. I couldn't see what it was, but I could feel its eyes on me. The sense of evil intent was nearly overwhelming, and I wanted out from under its gaze.

After the deputy punched in a code on a little keypad, we entered, leaving whatever was watching out in the dark. The lock reengaged with a click as the door swung closed, securing us inside. The bumps on my arms remained, nonetheless.

— • ● • —

Journal Excerpt

If you're reading this and you aren't me, then you have my journal. I wrote it for my own purposes. If you have it, I don't know why. Perhaps I didn't survive.

Or I did, and I'm sharing the story with you. Either way, just know there are things,

dangerous things, lurking in the night.

Two

Journal Excerpt

Gator Randall is an odd name, but who am I to judge?

At least he doesn't have to check a notebook every day to remember who he is.

———•●•———

A few minutes later, I sat down on a metal chair with a thin layer of vinyl-covered foam pretending to be a cushion; it was positioned parallel to a steel desk. The workstation carried a computer terminal along with various random papers.

Deputy Randall handed me a chilled bottle of water he'd pulled from a small refrigerator in one of the corners. "Thank you," I barely sputtered before guzzling the liquid. "I was really thirsty," I added with a sigh as I lowered the container.

"I see that." The deputy sat at the desk, facing me on an angle. He smiled. Neatly trimmed whiskers covered his jawline. I got a genuine vibe.

"So, have you remembered who you are yet?" he asked.

"Well, no, but maybe my journal will tell us." I remembered seeing it earlier while rummaging in the bag. Even if I didn't recall much of what it contained, I knew it was mine.

"Pull it out and let's have a look."

The pack was at my feet. Deputy Randall waited patiently as I unzipped the compartment and retrieved the spiral-bound notebook. It was thick, about an inch deep in paper. The red plastic wire at the binding extended out from the bottom a couple of turns. Someone, me I guess, had doodled drawings across the cover—stick figures and random geometric shapes that wouldn't win a kindergartener any awards. Moving a tad slow, I opened to the first page. Someone, me again I suppose, had scrawled a sentence across the top:

Your Name is D.R. Moon.

I turned the notebook so the deputy could see it.

"Did you write that?"

"I dunno," I said, and I really didn't.

He handed me a pen and his own notepad. "Try writing it; see if it matches."

I did, and it did. "I guess that's me, then. I'm D.R. Moon."

"Doctor Moon," Randall stated. "Has a ring to it." He laughed. "Kinda fitting, too, since I found you in the moonlight giving a local bully a treatment of sorts." He laughed again.

"I think those are just initials," I said, squinting at the paper. "I don't know for sure, but I don't think I'm an actual doctor."

"No, I suppose not. You look like you're in your late teens or early twenties. No way you've gone to medical school, yet. But 'Doc' is as good a nickname as any, at least until we figure out what your full name really is."

I stared at him, not knowing what to say, although I kind of liked the nickname.

"Anything else in that book of yours that'll give us

any hints?"

Looking down, I studied the page. "It says I'm supposed to go to Sarasota, Florida."

"Why is that?"

"It doesn't say. See?" I turned the journal toward him again.

You are to walk to Sarasota, Florida. Take your time.

The journey is as important as the destination.

Your instincts will guide your mission.

Follow them, and you'll get where you need to be.

The same handwriting. I must've written that also.

"Does it say where you come from or how long you've been on the road? Your scruffy face says you haven't shaved in a few days. You're thin but not starving."

"I am sorta hungry."

"I might have a candy bar in this desk somewhere." The deputy started rustling around, opening and closing drawers. He found a Snickers in the one on the lower right and handed it to me.

I tore open the wrapper and took a bite as I flipped through the pages, fanning them with my thumb. "It doesn't say when or where I started, but I've only written on about a quarter of the sheets." I studied a couple of the early pages more closely. "Most of the entries don't say where I was. It says I was in Terre Haute a couple pages back, but nothing happened there that I wrote about. None of the pages are dated. As I think about it, I don't even know what today's date is."

"June 21st. First day of summer."

"Okay. Thanks," I said.

"Actually, it's the 22nd now. Why don't you let me study that journal for a few minutes? Maybe something will catch my eye."

I handed it over, and after a few minutes of watching his eyes scan the pages, I stood and wandered around the office, chewing the candy as I went. There was a receiving counter in a corner across the room, near the front of the building. Along the opposite side wall was the most prominent desk in the room, stacked with papers in various boxes. A radio set rested on a rear credenza. I found a closed door with the label of "Sheriff Anders." Although I didn't recall if I'd been in other police stations, this one didn't seem all that remarkable.

I was standing before a bulletin board pinned with missing persons when Deputy Randall interrupted my thoughts. "A few of these notes tell some crazy stories, Doc," he said, as he approached and handed my journal back to me. "Seems like you've been through some messes. If everything in there is true, some of the stories are really strange. You don't remember any of it?"

"Not a bit. Does it say where all those messes happened?"

"Nope. And, it doesn't say when, either. There's nothing in there that I can trace."

"Maybe I should start writing in the names of places and the dates, too." I took the notebook, pulled the pen from one of the side pockets of my cargo pants, and scribbled a note on the next blank page to remind me to do just that. "Seems like something I should've thought of already." I shook my head. "But who knows what I've been thinking, right?"

The deputy smiled and nodded. "Memory issues can be a bugger, I suppose."

"What's the name of this town? I saw it on the sign as I walked by, but I want to make sure I spell it right. Cutters something, right?"

"Cutters Notch. No apostrophe."

"Excellent," I said, then I found the next blank

page and scribbled it across the top.

I pointed at the bulletin board. "Seems like you have a lot of missing people around here. How recent are they?" There were five photos. One on the left and four on the right. A string pinned to the top divided the board into two sections. My instinct was ringing my curiosity bell.

"The one on the left is old, over twenty years ago. Could even be thirty years. I've lost track." He pointed at the photo of a bushy-headed guy with a mustache and chin beard. "The four on the right are brand new. They all disappeared within the last month, starting with this guy." Randall tapped a photo of a middle-aged man with a balding head of light brown hair and a scruffy, round face. "Dave Kurz. He wasn't from around here, but his flatbed truck was found abandoned at the Quarry Pit, the local diner.

"Dig the food," I mumbled.

"What?"

"Nothing. I saw the motto on their sign. Guess I'm still hungry."

Deputy Randall paused. "I don't have anything else. You'll have to wait for breakfast. I'm sorry."

"I'll be okay," I confirmed.

"Anyway," Randall continued to tell the missing man's story, "we found his phone in the weeds along Bluff Road by pinging his GPS. Got it right before it ran out of juice. But we found no sign of the man himself."

"Bluff Road?"

"The road that winds up to the top of the cliff that overlooks the town. It starts down there by the General, the little store, but it runs the opposite direction from Robbins Creek Road." The only thing I recognized in that whole explanation was the General Store, where I pulled the old Twinkies from the trash.

"And the other three?" My curiosity was working

overtime as I studied the photos of two girls and one guy. Something compelled me to learn more. Not your run-of-the-mill compulsion like you're yearning for French fries. No, this was more like my mind would explode if I didn't learn more about this whole story.

"One disappearance per week since the Kurz guy vanished. The town is on edge, especially anyone living alone. Cutters Notch is small, Doc. Most people know one another, so if someone disappears, it affects almost everyone. Now we have three locals gone. We've had our share of strange occurrences over the years, but it's been a while, so the people are rattled."

"They look young," I mumbled. "All but the first guy," I added with more volume, now tapping Kurz's photo with my finger.

"Yeah. The two girls are teenagers. The guy is a little older, maybe about your age. He's twenty-two."

"No clues?"

"No, but there were a few similarities. They were all alone, and they were taken at night. Jason, the twenty-two-year-old, had a flat tire along Bluff Road. We found his car but no sign of him. The two girls— one sixteen and one seventeen—were both walking home after dark from a friend's house— each alone. And before you ask, it was a different friend's house each time. No connection."

"When was the last one taken?"

"About a week ago."

My brain formed the image of a calendar divided by weeks. Each missing person's face was in a square— one week apart for four weeks in a row. "So, if you follow the pattern, you're due to lose another person any day now."

Deputy Randall stared at me. Then he stared for a long time at the pictures on the board. No words passed his lips for maybe a minute while he contemplated what

I'd just said. Finally, he spoke. "Let's hope not, Doc." He placed his hand on my shoulder and turned me back toward the office.

I yawned. "I'm really tired. Is there somewhere I could crash for a couple of hours?"

"Sure." Randall walked me down a hallway to a block of open cells. "You can take whichever one you want. There's a cabinet at the end of the hall with fresh clothes and some towels. Why don't you change out of what you're wearing and take a shower. I'll run your clothes through the wash. They'll be fresh and clean when you wake up. Just leave 'em on the floor here in the hallway. I'll get to 'em in a few minutes."

"I'd appreciate that—" I offered a weak smile; it was the best I could do. "But why are you helping me so much?" Then I yawned again.

"Years ago, I moved away from home for a few years. I tried baseball, and that didn't work out. Anyway, long story short, I found myself without a home for a little while. Some folks helped me. Now, I pay it forward whenever I can."

A tiny tear escaped and moistened his cheek as Deputy Randall spoke, his eyes distant as he remembered his past. His jaw was working overtime to control his emotions. "Go on then and get some sleep," he finally managed to say. "When you wake up, come on out to the office." He motioned back the way we'd come. "Either I'll still be sitting at my desk, or the morning team will be coming in around seven."

"I'm not under arrest, right?"

He chuckled. "No. Why would you be? You probably saved Joanie from getting a serious whooping. If that had happened, she'd be on her way to the hospital in French Lick, if Ronnie didn't accidentally kill her, and Ronnie himself would be getting locked in that cell you're about to sleep in. You saved me a whole lot of trouble—and paperwork. I'm grateful—another good reason to help you out."

"What if you get another call?"

"Unlikely." He lifted his brown hat and scratched the back of his head. "If I do, I'll let you know." Then he left me alone in front of the metal bars and headed back toward the office.

I meandered to the cabinet containing the fresh clothes. Scrubs. Orange. I may not be under arrest, but I'd look like it for a few hours. After showering, donning the colorful duds, and hitting the men's room, I pulled back the sheets on the bunk inside the first cell, grateful to have something comfortable to sleep on— more comfortable than pine needles anyway. It wasn't a fancy hotel mattress, but it sure beat the top of a picnic table, or a bed of oily rags in someone's shed.

For a few minutes, I sat up, leaning against the concrete wall, and added several notes to the new "Cutters Notch" section in my journal. I add notes often during the days so I can keep ahead of the black monster that eats my memories.

Eventually, when I dropped my head on the pillow, staring at the ceiling with everything quiet, there it was again, that ominous sense of darkness. There was something bad in this town. Something caused those teens to go missing. That same something had been watching me, too. I didn't see it, but I felt it. Perhaps, it was a good thing for me that I'd run into Ronnie. Maybe being alone at night in Cutters Notch, Indiana, wasn't a very good idea.

I fell asleep to the sound of the cool air blowing through a vent hanging from the ceiling in the hallway. I slept well except for the yellow eyes that kept intruding into my mind.

Three

Journal Excerpts

Something dangerous is preying upon this town. It takes lone victims in the night.

I know I'm going to Sarasota, Florida, but I don't know why.

I feel like my life is an erased page, not knowing where I'm from or who I am.

Where did I grow up? Who are my parents? Are they alive?

Deputy Randall gave me a nickname. He's calling me Doc.

* * *

Angry words echoing down the hallway awakened me—a female sobbing and a male making accusations. I couldn't make out the details. While I was curious, as usual, I didn't find it especially alarming. I was in a sheriff's office, after all. Then, the stuff still existing in my short-term memory flooded back. My mental calendar reformed behind my eyes, depicting the missing people—all taken one week apart. One week had passed since the last disappearance. Based on the pattern, another person was due to go missing. Dread gripped my heart, driving me to my feet.

I'd slept well but it was morning. Sunlight shone through the windows spaced along the top edge of the hallway. Morning rays illuminated the dust motes floating inside my cell. I stretched and found my shoes.

After stopping again in the men's room to splash my face with some water and rinse my mouth, I cautiously headed toward the main office. Since my orange trousers were a tad loose, I held them up as I walked.

"There he is! That's the guy." Ronnie, in a fresh T-shirt and a pair of jeans, pointed at me from where he stood at a desk across the room. Joanie, her hair brushed and tied back in a ponytail, was slumped in the chair beside the workspace, sobbing. "He chased her across the park and right up into her mom's house. He's some sort of weird pervert."

Everyone in the room turned to stare at me. Deputy Randall stood at the reception counter. A deputy I didn't know sat at the desk where the domestically-challenged couple hurled accusations in my direction. An older woman was nestled behind the paper-strewn desk with the radio base station on the credenza to her rear. A large man, the sheriff I presumed, stood in a doorway next to the nameplate labeled *Sheriff Anders*. They all followed Ronnie's pointed finger to find my sunburnt, unshaven face.

I looked at the clock hanging on the wall above the reception desk. Seven a.m. Best night's sleep I'd had in a while. Of course, that was just a guess, since I couldn't remember how I'd slept previously. For the moment, I could still remember the previous day's breakfast, which made me hungry again.

The way things were starting, today looked like it was going to be an interesting day. With the death vision still fresh in my mind, I knew I had a lot to look forward to before the 22nd of June was finished.

"Ronnie, it wasn't him," Gator calmly said.

"It was. It had to be," Ronnie spat. "Who else could it be? He's the only stranger in town."

"He was here with me all night. Sleeping in your favorite cell down the hall."

"Gator, we don't need your sarcasm," snapped the sheriff.

"Sorry, Rick, but Doc couldn't have done it. I'm telling you he was asleep right down the hall. I even looked in on him a few times. He never moved. Slept like a baby all night."

Ronnie glared at me, nonetheless. He obviously wasn't over our little introduction from last night. Maybe I wasn't the guy, but he sure wanted me to be.

"Well, now that we've got that cleared up—" the woman behind the paper piles said as she stood, "let's make some introductions. I'm Judy Steinkamp. You know Gator over there." She nodded toward where he stood. "That's Deputy Calvin Churchill taking statements." Churchill peered up and waved. "And that's our sheriff, Rick Anders, standing in the doorway there."

"Your name's Doc?" Sheriff Anders asked as he walked over and extended his hand for a shake.

"Good a name as any, I guess," I replied. "That's what Deputy Randall is calling me. All I know is my name is D.R. Moon."

"Doc it is then," Anders said. "Welcome to Cutters Notch. Gator tells me you drifted into town last night. He said he took you in here to keep you from sleeping in the park. Gator's got a bad habit of taking in strays. Regardless, he's vouched for you, so we'll be hospitable. If you want some coffee, there's a pot brewing in the breakroom." He pointed past me toward the back hallway.

"Your clothes are all washed up and fresh, too," Gator added. "You grab your coffee, and I'll fetch your clothes."

As I headed toward the breakroom, I heard the attention turn back to Ronnie and Joanie. Taking my time, I was careful to be quiet. I wanted to hear the story.

Deputy Churchill prompted the girl. "Come on now, Joanie. Tell me the story. We know it wasn't Doc, so what the blazin' rabbit bones happened?"

As I slowly poured my coffee, mixed with a generous portion of sugar and some powdered creamer, Joanie began the tale. I eased back to the doorframe and listened in.

"Ronnie and me, we'd been fighting all night. He was fixing to get rough again—"

"I was not," Ronnie blurted.

"You were. You know you were. Anyway, he went to the bathroom, and I slipped out the front door. My momma lives on the far side of the park, so I was cutting across when I heard a stick snap in the grass behind me. I figured it was Ronnie, so I turned around to tell him to leave me alone and…and…" She started gasping for breath.

The deputy was patient. He let the girl gather herself. "It's okay, Joanie. You're safe now. What time was it when you were going across the park?"

"It was a couple hours ago. About five, I guess. The sky was starting to glow over the treetops."

"What'd you see when you turned around?"

"I dunno exactly. A man. He was all dark. His eyes were weird. Yellow. And he didn't blink. I just panicked and ran. Heard his footsteps behind me until I reached the porch. My mom's an early bird, or he would've gotten me. I banged on the door. She flipped on the light and opened up right away. I could see him through the window after she locked us inside. He was fluttering through the park toward the bluff."

"Fluttering?"

She was quiet for a moment. "Yeah, weird, huh? He was fluttering. Like some sort of bird."

"Here's your clothes." Deputy Randall interrupted my eavesdropping session. He held a green plastic laundry basket. My duds were folded in the bottom. "After you change, drop the orange things in the basket and leave it in the hallway. We'll take care of 'em."

"Thank you, Deputy," I said.

"Call me Gator. We can be less formal now."

"Thanks, Gator."

"I'm headed home. My shift's over, and I've gotta sleep sometime. I've asked the sheriff to get you some breakfast. He's not as tough on the inside as he seems on the outside." He stuck out his hand. "Nice to meet you, kid."

I shook his hand. "Nice to meet you, too. Thanks for the sleeping space."

"Not a problem and you're welcome." He lightly slapped my shoulder, smiled, and headed to the back door.

—•●•—

I changed into my regular clothes. Not knowing what else to do, I returned to the cell, sat on the bed, and reviewed my journal, placing additional memories of the previous couple of days back into my mind. Taking my pen, I updated my notebook on the events of the previous night, including that vision that nearly rocked me off my feet, and Joanie's story of the fluttering birdman.

I thought about my bloody vision, perhaps a premonition of my own death, and I thought about that dark, yellow-eyed man in the park. Was there a connection? It was too soon to tell. Apparently, whatever or whoever was taking the missing young people in Cutters Notch had missed last night unless someone else came up missing. Would I be this week's victim? For the first time that day, leaving town crossed my mind.

"You hungry, Doc?" Sheriff Anders stepped into the cell's doorframe. His large torso threw a shadow over my writings.

That was an easy question to answer. "Yessir. Famished."

"Come on, then. We'll go down to the Quarry Pit and get you fixed up. Best breakfast in a thirty-mile radius." He smiled as he put his hat over his crewcut and then hiked up his utility belt. "I'm not usually this generous to strange men who wander in during the night, but Gator's buying. Besides, it'll give me a chance to size you up."

It made sense for him to be a touch suspicious of me. I didn't mind. I may not be the one who chased Joanie, but I was still a stranger in town. "Lead the way, Sheriff. I'm an open book, but unfortunately most of the pages are blank right now."

Moments later, I slipped into the passenger side of the sheriff's car. The sheriff himself filled the driver's seat, and we headed to breakfast. The sun was already well into the sky, spraying the trees and various buildings with rays of light that sparkled on the dew leftover from the previous night. Even the sprawling scrapyard across the road almost looked pretty under the morning sun. As I stared at it, that familiar yearning pulled me toward the piles of twisted metal. Something wanted me to come that way. It felt like a call for help.

I gazed at the tall chain-link fence as it whirred past. The spikes of the barbed wire along the top looked ominous. The twirls were interspersed with more dangerous razor wire. Climbing over that fence would be a truly stupid idea.

A man stood inside the gate, hands at his sides, staring out. His eyes met mine, his bushy head of hair, mustache, and chin beard emanating a faint glow. It was the man from the bulletin board—the one who'd disappeared twenty or thirty years ago. My eyes followed his form as we traveled beyond him, and he soon faded from view. He had to be the one beckoning me to come help.

"Gator told me about all the people that've disappeared in the last few weeks. We were looking at the pictures on the board last night."

Sheriff Anders left me hanging. No response at all. As I glanced his way, worry lines crinkled his forehead. A slight grimace replaced his previous smile. I'd touched on a painful point.

"That's a pretty crazy story that girl told this morning," I added.

"It is," he replied.

"Yet, nobody seemed too surprised."

"Doc," he said as he slowed to enter the diner's parking lot, "this place has a habit of finding itself in the middle of crazy stories. From kidnappings to cannibalistic killers to bigfoot, I'm afraid it takes quite a bit to rattle us."

I wondered about all that but didn't pursue it. "Can you tell me about the old missing-person case? Gator said it was from over twenty, maybe even thirty years ago."

"It'll be thirty years later this summer. I'll tell you what I can over breakfast." He held the door for me as we entered, then pointed to a booth in the corner. "Hey, Roger," he called out to someone.

"Mornin', Rick," the guy behind the grill replied.

"What's shakin' this bright day?"

We paused by the counter. "Been meaning to ask you about Josh. Has he picked his college yet?" asked the sheriff.

"Not yet," answered the cook with a white grease-stained apron hanging off his neck. Middle-aged. Medium-length dark hair with a little gray on the sides. "I think he's leaning toward IU. That's the last I heard."

"Beautiful campus," Rick quipped. "I should've figured that since Hope's there. She hadn't said anything, though."

"They're still two peas in a pod. Three peas, really. I think Danny's headed there, too. If that happens, that place won't know what hit it." The grill master laughed, then returned to his work as we took our seats. The whole conversation lost me.

As we sat down, a blonde waitress approached wearing a light pink uniform with a white ruffle trim at the sleeves and neck. The hem of the skirt ended at her knees. "Mornin', Rick. Good morning, Doc."

"Do you know me?" How could she know me? I just got into town. Maybe this was my chance to connect with someone from my past. For a moment, my heart leapt. Sheriff Anders chuckled.

"Doc, this is Rhonda Randall. She's Gator's wife."

I tried hard not to show my disappointment. After all, it was nice to meet my new friend's bride. I gave her the best smile I could muster. "Good morning, Mrs. Randall," I told her.

"Call me Rhonda. Would you like some coffee?" She dropped two menus on the table. Her smile was sweet with her pink cheeks matching her lipstick.

The sheriff took the corner seat. "Yes, ma'am," he replied as his eyes scanned the room. "Glass of water, too, please."

She peered at me. "Same for me," I said.

"Thanks."

I had my back to the restaurant, so my view was Anders and the windows. Rather than stare at the sheriff, I gazed into the morning. Another gate to the junkyard was across the road. The man with the bushy head of hair again stared at me through the gate. I could feel his call inside my mind from across the highway. Apparently, he'd waited thirty years for someone to come along who could see him, and he wasn't going to let up until I responded.

Trying to be nonchalant, I picked up the menu and scanned it as I probed again for details. "What's the story on the guy who went missing way back when?"

"What's your interest, kid?"

"Beats me." I know. I say that a lot, but with no memory, stuff really does beat me. That said, I wasn't quite ready to fess up to the fact that I could see an apparition of the missing man standing in the junkyard across the road. "Something about looking at his face in the picture, I guess. I'm curious. Must be in my nature."

"All I know are some facts I looked up after I became sheriff. It happened a long time ago. Long before I even moved here."

Rhonda dropped off the coffee. "What can I getcha to eat?" she asked as I tore open a couple sugar packets. The sheriff ordered first. He didn't need a menu.

"Two eggs, scrambled. Bacon, crispy, as usual. Some hashbrowns. And…a side of rye toast with lots of butter. I'm a little hungry today." He smiled.

"Honey, you're hungry like this every day."

Pink tips contrasted with Rhonda's blonde locks as she turned slightly to take my order. "I'll have the same thing," I said. "Sounds wonderful."

"You got it," she said as she turned away. Then she began to rattle off the orders to Roger in the kitchen using diner jargon I didn't understand.

Sheriff Anders rubbed his face. Then he stared out the window for a few moments. I guess he was gathering the details in his mind. "It was summer. A hot August, I'm told. Jasper Fresno was his name. He lived alone in a shack a little east of town, just inside the county line. He was kind of a loner, they say. Anyway, he'd gone to French Lick to get some part for his truck."

"French Lick?"

The sheriff laughed. "Yeah, I know, sounds like a…well, anyway, it's another town a few miles away." I chuckled, too, but I wasn't sure why it was funny.

"Apparently, he bought the part he needed around closing time. The clerk said he left the store at about nine p.m. Said he was headed back toward Cutters Notch. Thing is, he never made it. They never found him or his truck. It's like he drove off the face of the Earth."

I glanced out the window again. Jasper Fresno's image was no longer standing inside the gate of the scrapyard, but I was pretty sure I knew where he and his truck had ended up. There could be no other reason why his ghost was beckoning me to visit him inside the piles of junked cars.

"Did he have friends? Enemies?" I was looking for other details, clues.

"Like I said, they say he was a loner. From what I'm told, he was a grumpy fella. Not many folks liked being around him, so he kept pretty much to himself."

I considered the story as I sipped my coffee. August. After nine p.m. It wouldn't be dark yet, but it would be approaching dusk. A county highway. His truck was already having issues. It was thirty years ago, but people still had cell phones, even in those dark ages. I'm not sure how I know that, but I do. It's like one of those facts hanging on the nonexistent whiteboard in my head. Anyway, he must have called a tow truck. But what happened then? I didn't know yet, but I knew I'd have to visit that junkyard across the road to see if I could find out.

Our breakfast arrived—one plate for the sheriff and one plate for me. His plate had four slices of bacon, mine had two. "What's up with that?" I asked Anders, pointing at his extra bounty.

He smiled. "It pays to be in good with the cook."

The food was delicious. I couldn't remember ever having anything better. Seriously. I couldn't remember. The previous day's breakfast was now erased.

I shifted gears to the more recent cases. "Gator said the new disappearances started with a guy named Kurz. His truck was found in the lot right outside?" I shoved some egg onto my fork with some buttered toast and filled my mouth while the sheriff spoke.

"Roger, the owner—he's the cook back there—" Anders pointed over my shoulder. "Well, he found it parked alongside the building when he opened up one morning. Rhonda recognized it when she came in for the lunch crowd. She told us it belonged to a guy who'd eaten a late dinner there the previous evening, but he'd left with it when they were closing up. No one knows how it ended up parked back in the lot."

Rhonda came strolling by to refill the coffee cups. "How's the food, boys?"

"Delicious," I said. "I don't know when I've ever eaten something so good." That was the truth.

"Rhonda," Anders interrupted, "Doc wants to know about the guy who disappeared a few weeks back, leaving his truck outside."

She perched the coffee urn in one cocked arm and leaned with her other hand on her hip. With a thoughtful pucker, she nodded. "He came in late, around eight o'clock. Sorta gruff, thin hair combed over a balding head. Tan skin, like he was in the sun a lot. Said he was in town to drop off a shipping container on the bluff. He wanted to grab something to eat before heading home."

"Shipping container?" I asked.

"You know, one of those large, rectangular metal boxes they ship stuff in from around the world."

"Nope. Not familiar to me." That detail wasn't on the whiteboard.

She continued, "Anyway, he sat at the counter, head down, munching on a burger and fries with black coffee, when all at once, he let out a curse. He said something about how he'd forgotten to unlock the container before he left. Something else about how it had to be opened before it got dark, or he wouldn't get paid. He tossed down a twenty, rushed out, jumped in the truck, and sped off toward town. By then, it was nine o'clock and time to close up."

"Was it dark, then?"

"No," the sheriff answered. "Not quite yet, but it was a month ago, so it was close. It would have been dusk, for sure."

"That's all I know," Rhonda said. She headed off to refill some more cups at the other end of the diner.

"Can you take me up on that bluff, Sheriff?"

"What are you? Some sort of amateur investigator?"

I shrugged.

Anders stared at me for a few seconds, considering the request. "You are an interesting character, Doc." He glanced at his watch. "Guess I have some free time this morning. I need to stop and chat with Joanie's mom in a few minutes, but it can't hurt anything to show you around first. Let's take a ride, and you can have a look."

Four

Journal Excerpts

Ronnie is still angry at me. Joanie was chased through the park by a fluttering man with yellow eyes. Was he the lurking evil I sensed?

Apparently, I can see ghosts. His name is Jasper. He doesn't feel evil.

The missing Kurz dude was upset because he forgot to unlock a container that he'd delivered nearby.

If he didn't open it before dark, he wouldn't get paid.

— • ● • —

The ride began with a stop at The General. "Coffee," Anders explained.

"Didn't you just have two cups at the diner?"

"Gotta keep the tank full. And, well, empty the tank, too."

He strolled inside with me on his heels and headed straight to the men's room. I stopped to browse. The counter was to the right with a wall of tobacco products as a backdrop. Coolers lined the left side and back walls. The coffee station was straight ahead. "Get what you want," he instructed before closing the restroom door. "I'm buying."

He didn't have to tell me twice. As far as I knew, anyway. I found the Twinkie display and grabbed a couple of fresh packages. A few minutes later, I joined the sheriff at the coffee contraptions. "What's a cappuccino?" I asked. Perhaps, I'd drunk hundreds of them but had no memory of the experiences. The word meant nothing to me.

"Try one," Anders replied. "You'll like it. Go for the toffee flavor. That's my favorite."

I filled a tall cup and met up with him again at the register. A beautiful young brunette with freckles stood there waiting for us. She took the breath right out of me. Her badge gave her name: *Rose*. She smiled. "Mornin', sunshine," she said to Anders. Her hair fell in waves across the sides of her face, draping her shoulders. Her lips were full, and her green eyes sparkled.

I thought I'd fallen in love but maybe smitten is a better word. Did I mention she was beautiful? She didn't look that much older than me, maybe two or three years—definitely within my age range. Then I remembered my scruffy face, long hair, and ragged clothes. At least I'd taken a shower the previous night, and my clothes were clean.

"Good morning, Rose," Anders said. "How's business?"

"A little early to tell. Is that the 'Doc' kid with you?"

Small town. Word gets around. "That's me," I replied for myself. "I take it Gator's been here, too." She smiled and gave me a cute little wink. I'm pretty sure I blushed. As I looked down, a smile wrapped across my face. I had to turn away to hide my embarrassingly flushed cheeks. To get my heart under control, I directed my eyes to the world outside the plate-glass windows.

Across the road and slightly to the right was the drive that led to the house with the "come-visit" vibe. Right now, it was putting out a "leave-her-alone" vibe. That was a definite change of tone. I don't know why or how I feel these things. Every time feels like the first time, so I wasn't sure how to react.

When I felt more in control, I turned back to soak in more of her beauty. "You live across the street, right?" I asked. "That's your driveway right there. Am I right?"

Her eyes went wide. "Well, yeah," she said. "Big house back behind the trees. You noticed it?"

"Sure." I didn't elaborate. "It's hard to miss."

"People—even people who've lived here for years—don't notice it's there. How'd you know I live there?" Her eyes narrowed. Then she glanced at the sheriff for a moment before refocusing on me. "Seriously. How did you know?"

"I seem to notice things other people don't. And it's like the house just told me to leave you alone. I felt it. It's claimed you." Immediately, I felt I'd said too much. I'd just told the most beautiful girl I could ever remember seeing that I heard houses speaking to me.

As I spoke, her eyes softened. "I've claimed it, too." She smiled again, accepting my explanation as if it happened all the time. "We have a very long history. If the house is letting you see it, then there's no reason for me to be concerned."

It seemed as if Sheriff Anders couldn't hear our words. If he could, he didn't react at all, despite the weirdness of the conversation.

"Last night, it was telling me to come visit. I guess it's changed its mind."

"That's interesting." Rose gazed through the window toward her house. "I'm intrigued. Even my own brother can't find my house. Maybe you should...come visit." She winked again. "After all, if the house likes you, then I don't see any reason why we can't be friends."

"Let's take that ride up Bluff Road," Anders suddenly interjected. "Time's ticking away, and I've got an appointment with Joanie's mom. You never know, maybe you'll see something with those fresh eyes of yours." As I glanced toward the sheriff, I sensed sincerity in his words. He wasn't just humoring me.

As we headed toward the door, Rose came around the counter. "Will you still be in town around lunchtime?" She was fingering her throat as if playing with a necklace that wasn't there. Her fingers were slender with red polish on the nails.

"Dunno," I answered, pausing as Anders exited first. "I suppose so."

"Come back by. My morning shift ends at noon. I'll fix you some lunch, and you can see the house." She winked once more. Blood rushed to my face again.

Anders leaned back in. "Where do you live again, Rose?" he asked.

"Right there, Rick." She pointed across the road. Looking me in the eyes, she added, "He won't remember. No one ever does. It's the house."

I was still thinking about Rose, the house, and the strange vibes as Sheriff Anders wheeled off the lot. My head turned to catch another glimpse of Rose. I couldn't help myself.

"She's too old for you, kid," Anders said.

"I wasn't thinking about that," I lied.

"Yes, you were. I'm observant for a living, and I saw how your eyes were following her. I don't know exactly how old she is, but she hides it extremely well. I'm guessing she's about forty—roughly twice your age." He smiled and pointed his cruiser uphill, away from Cutters Notch.

Forty years old? Impossible. Still, I sensed only sincerity from Anders. This place was turning out to be a strange little town, but then again, my memory didn't have much to compare it to. Maybe I was just a poor judge of age.

"This road has a different name on the other side of the light?" I pointed with my thumb over my shoulder.

"Yep. It's Robbins Creek Road over there. Named after the Robbins family. Back in the day, they pretty much built this town. It was the money coming from their stone quarries that funded most of the older infrastructure. They're all gone now, except for one old man, Willie Robbins. He lives in a farmhouse a couple miles back that way." Anders motioned over his shoulder the same way I had. "He's my neighbor. Kind of eccentric."

"What's up on top?" I pointed at the ridge we were winding our way towards. Bluff Road followed a serpentine course through tall trees and lots of undergrowth, going ever upward. Here and there stood large, rectangularly-cut stones sitting back in the trees. I couldn't see much past the end of the hood.

Sheriff Anders rubbed his clean-shaven chin. "Not much. Some fenced-off, abandoned industrial properties. Mostly remnants of the mining industry. When I moved here, I was surprised no one had built any houses up there, but, as it turns out, all the rich folk had built their mansions down at the base of the bluff."

"Like the one Rose lives in?"

"Which one is she in again?" Anders asked. I glanced at him to see if he was serious. He was. Weird. "I can't ever seem to hold onto that detail."

"She just told us. The one that sits diagonally across from her store. You could almost throw a rock and hit it."

"Oh, yeah. For some reason, I seem to forget as fast as she tells me."

I stared at him as we turned onto another switchback. Although I might have very little memory to pull from, this place seemed awfully strange. I did remember walking through a couple of little towns the day before—they hadn't dropped from my memory yet—but they couldn't hold a candle to Cutters Notch when it came to weirdness.

The road angled up sharply as we made the last turn, then flattened out to parallel the cliff edge as we headed east. The berm on the right was only wide enough to accommodate a vehicle. A steel guardrail lined the space to keep anyone from accidentally driving off and landing on one of the big houses down below. It made me wonder if that'd ever happened. Here and there some huge trees—oaks, maples, and sycamores—provided shade for the narrow lane winding along the edge.

"Quite a view," Anders commented. "Never gets old. Before I got married a few years back, I used to come up here at night and gaze at the stars over the trees." He was shooting quick glances as he drove along.

By now, the sun was high in the sky, and I could see off to the right for miles and miles. The sea of green spread in all directions. Occasionally, individual trees stood like sentinels above the others, representing an even older age of the forest. I could see the highway below as it passed through the other end of Cutters Notch and wound through the trees like a snake. Birds floated on the currents, performing slow, observant loops above the canopy.

On my left was a ten-foot-high chain-link fence with three strands of barbed wire strung along the top. Metal plates were attached at intervals. "Keep Out," they ordered. "No Trespassing." Along the fence grew a smattering of scrub brush and young trees, much younger than the forest below. Dilapidated sheds and industrial buildings, partially hidden by weeds, stood back at a distance. All visible windows were broken or boarded up.

It was odd, the disparity of the landscape. To the right, a wide-open expanse of beautiful forest flowing for miles and miles—nature, for the most part, untouched. To the left, wire, weeds, and waste—Mother Nature trying to reclaim what was rightfully hers.

"Did you ever figure out where Kurz delivered the…what'd you call it? The shipping container?"

"We looked around, but nothing stood out. There was no sign of it."

"If it had to be delivered on a flatbed truck, it'd be pretty large, right?" My eyes darted between the abandoned buildings and the scrub brush behind the chain-link fence. Somewhere beyond the fence seemed to be the most logical location for something large to be delivered.

"They're huge. We should've been able to see the container, as big as it is," said the sheriff.

I fell silent. Thinking. Looking around. After a moment, I had another question. "Did you go inside the old industrial buildings?"

"We couldn't. It's private property, locked behind gates, and we didn't have a warrant or any probable cause. We tried to reach the owners to get permission, but it's some company in New York. They didn't return our calls."

I fell silent again. Anders was creeping along. The slow speed let me have a good look around, not only at the bluff up here, but also at the town and surrounding forest down below. It was a spectacular view.

"Ahead is the lone house on the ridge," Anders announced. "As far as I know, it was the only one ever built up here." The sheriff pointed to the right as the road curved to the left. Bluff Road wrapped around the property that contained a large Victorian home nestled right up against the edge of the cliff. A black wrought-iron fence, overgrown with weeds and vines, surrounded the grounds.

We approached an entrance drive to what was once likely the most valuable estate in the area. A rusty gate blocked the compacted gravel lane, secured with a chain and padlock. The stone house sat toward the back of the property and featured two major wings, one on each side, with ornate trim and fine details, albeit with chipping paint and rusted metal. Vines had also grown up the sides of the structure, covering several windows and hanging off the roof and gutters.

The drive curled past the wide front porch before winding around the far side to an oversized garage, also with neglected ornate trim. A cupola sprouted out the top of the garage with windows all around. No glass remained in any of the frames.

"Wow, that's an amazing place," I said. "I'm literally shaking with excitement. Seems I really like old houses." I really was shaking. I couldn't keep my hands still. Even my shoulders were vibrating. For some reason, my body shot me full of adrenaline again.

"Yeah, me too," Anders added with a smile. "They don't build 'em like that anymore."

The sheriff came to a stop before the gate so I could get a good look. I got more than a view as I gazed up into the house's dark windows. They stared back at me like evil eyes. Suddenly I was hit with psychic energy that pinned me back to my seat, consuming all my thoughts. Images shot across my brain like a big screen movie, complete with sound. I squeezed my eyes shut, trying to block the incoming waves of data.

———•●•———

When I reopened my eyes, my view was someone else's vision. I was behind the wheel of a truck, sitting in front of the same gate. The radio was on, playing a country tune, Glen Campbell crooning about a lineman from the county. I could see hands not my own—hands that were large with calloused fingers. I tried to raise one for a better look, but I had no control. It seemed I was just along for the ride.

I grabbed a set of keys from the console and jumped out, leaving the vehicle running. Rounding to the gate, I unlocked it and swung it open on rusted, creaking hinges. A breeze ruffled my hair. Bugs gathered in front of the truck's headlights.

I stood there for a moment, feeling a touch of fear. Peering to the west, the sky glowed red, and the top edge of the sun hung barely visible just above the forest canopy. I checked the road; it was quiet. No traffic.

The man whose eyes I was seeing through climbed back in the truck, drove past the front of the house, and approached the garage. A mosquito bit his arm; he swatted it. I felt the bite and the smack. It left a small dab of blood. Other mosquitoes buzzed around, fluttering through my line of sight.

He opened the oversized garage doors—double doors that hung from hinges on either side of the opening. They swung outward to reveal a huge, brown corrugated metal container resting inside the structure. There was a name I didn't recognize printed in large, bold white letters across the container's doors.

The house cast a deep shadow over the garage opening. I could only see because of the truck's lights. The man retrieved a pair of bolt cutters from behind the driver's seat. I watched as he used them to snip a couple metal bands that secured the door mechanism on the container. That left a padlock.

I could feel the fear rising inside Dave Kurz. That's who he was. It had to be. I was an interloper, watching the events unfold through his eyes. He fumbled with a keychain, sorting the options as the light continued to fade. Finally, he found the right one, slipped it in the lock's key slot, and popped it free.

With no lock or seals, he was able to operate the latching mechanism on the container easily. He glanced over his shoulder at the fading sun, and a sense of relief washed over him as he pulled the door open a crack. Kurz had done it. He'd gotten it open before it was dark. Well, at least it wasn't completely dark. The purple in the western sky still indicated a touch of daylight. Kurz hoped it was enough to satisfy his employer.

He didn't look inside. Kurz's memories were my memories for the moment. The instructions he'd been given were clear. Deliver the container to the location. Place it inside the garage. Unseal and unlock the doors. Leave them open just a crack, but don't open them all the way. DO NOT LOOK INSIDE was printed in bold capital letters. Close the garage doors and leave. The paperwork indicated that if he failed to follow any of the instructions to the letter, his employer would know, and he would not get paid. If he followed the directions, money would appear in his bank account later that night. Ten thousand dollars on top of the five thousand he'd been fronted—a lot of money just to deliver one container.

How could his employer know? The place was vacant with no sign of electrical power. No lights anywhere. As I gazed through the man's eyes, he peered around the garage frame and across to the house. No cameras. There was no way for his employer to have any clue as to whether he followed every step.

This was all very weird, which raised the curiosity level in Dave Kurz's mind. DO NOT LOOK INSIDE— what a load of crap. The man's feeling of intense curiosity and a touch of defiance translated directly to me as I observed the experience like a rerun of a TV show broadcast through Kurz's eyes. The man had to find out what was inside; his curiosity was too intense to ignore.

Maybe if he'd left it alone. Maybe if he'd not retrieved the flashlight from his truck. Maybe if he'd simply done as he was told. If he'd not been so incredibly curious or so defiant. None of that mattered, though, because Dave Kurz was who Dave Kurz was.

In this case, curiosity killed the truck driver.

Flashlight in hand, he slowly swung the lefthand door outward. There was an odd odor, maybe like rotten corn. Stale and putrid. The light beam probed the darkness, touching the ceiling, the sidewalls, and the floor. Inside sat an array of old furniture. The pieces looked like antiques, arranged as if the container was a room in someone's home. Toward the back, the light caught a reflection. Two yellow dots that floated in the air.

Kurz squinted. "What is that?" he asked himself. Taking a step inside, he tried to adjust the beam on his Maglite. Then, he pointed again at the spot where the dots hung. They had moved. Closer.

"I told you to open the container before the sun set," a voice said. It carried an accent that I couldn't immediately place.

Kurz froze, his feet wouldn't move.

"I told you in no uncertain terms not to look inside. I told you I would know."

The truck driver jumped as his light beam landed on the face of his employer. All he saw were teeth—

long, jagged, and sharp. Kurz screamed, but the screaming stopped as those teeth closed around his throat.

———————•●•———————

I was screaming too, as Sheriff Anders grabbed hold of me in the front passenger seat of his cruiser. My arms were flailing, and my legs were kicking. If it weren't for the seatbelt holding me down, I may have flung myself through the windshield, and it was a good thing my cappuccino was safely in a cupholder. That was the second time I considered leaving Cutters Notch at my earliest opportunity.

"Doc! What's wrong?" Anders was trying to restrain me by pressing my shoulders to the seatback. Even as I calmed, the gleaming fangs hung in front of my eyes. My breaths were coming in bursts, and my heart was trying to hammer a hole through my ribcage.

"Oh, my God," I moaned. Kurz's terror was still palpable to me. It had traveled across time and space to land smack dab inside my psyche. I'd even felt the fangs penetrate Kurz's neck just before I snapped away from the scene.

"You zoned out. Your eyes went blank for a few seconds. Then, you went crazy, screaming and fighting at the air."

I stared at him, my arms and legs shaking. My blood surged through the arteries in my neck. The truck driver's death was raw in my memories. I'd literally seen it happen, just as much as if I'd been there. Hyperventilating, I closed my eyes and worked to calm my breathing.

"Has this kind of thing happened to you before?"

"I dunno. I don't remember. I sure hope it never

happens again."

"What was going on? Do you know? I thought you were having a seizure."

"Uhh…" I took another breath, trying to do it slowly. "I was seeing through Kurz's eyes." Turning back to face the old house, peering at its structure through the slats in the gate, I continued. "It happened here."

"What happened here?"

I took one more deep breath before starting the story. "It was dusk. He opened the shipping container. It was in the garage on the other side of the house." I pointed past the shrubbery. "It may still be there. He wasn't supposed to look inside, but he did anyway. Then—" I held my breath for a moment, trying to contain my physical reaction to the psychic visions. "Teeth. Yellow eyes and sharp, jagged teeth." I glanced back to the sheriff. "He's dead. There's no way he survived."

The sheriff exited the car. Reluctantly, I joined him on the gravel before the huge gate. He lifted the padlock, examining the clasp.

"Are you going in?" I asked.

"Can't. Don't have a warrant."

The vibes coming off the property were slamming into my already-shaken frame. Dark vibes. Evil but not defined. The vibes didn't form clear concepts like Rose's house. They only resounded in waves, sort of like heavy surf on a beach when a storm is looming offshore. Or, maybe, like deep breaths followed by the heavy snores of an unholy creature sleeping somewhere inside the Victorian mansion.

"If you get a warrant, do the search during the daylight. Don't be here after dark."

Five

Journal Excerpts

I met the girl of my dreams today. Beautiful. Young.

Reddish-brown hair and freckles. Her name is Rose.

Sheriff Anders says she's forty years old. I don't believe him.

Impossible.

The truck driver is dead. No way he survived. Curiosity killed him.

Yellow eyes, sharp teeth.

• ● •

We completed the cruise along Bluff Road, and the sheriff dropped me off at the park. He had an appointment to keep, and I thought a few minutes alone in the pleasant, shady surroundings would help calm my frayed nerves.

"You need anything?" Anders asked.

"No. I'm good."

"I'll be back at my office after lunch if you're still around."

"Sheriff?"

"Yeah?"

"That thing that killed Kurz is a monster, but it's intelligent. It spoke clearly. It even has an accent—European, I think. It understands and conducts business. It arranged the truck shipment that brought it here."

"You picked all that up in your vision?"

"I did."

"Okay. Good information to know," he said. "Thank you," he added before pulling away from the curb.

I turned toward the park. It seemed a little weird to have a rectangular section of trees situated in the middle of a small town that was already enveloped by a forest—a park inside a park. Huge, old trees with all the underbrush cleared out to make room for picnic tables, playgrounds, and concrete pavilions. A small road with parking slots along the edges wound through the center. It was quiet. Birds and squirrels were my only companions.

Four streets bordered the Cutters Notch Town Park. Rock Street to the west, Slab Street to the south, Boulder Street to the East, and I guess what they'd call Main Street to the north, but the only sign I could find just called it Highway 257. The three side streets all featured sweet little bungalows with well-kept yards, flowerpots, and aluminum siding. Each house sat up three steps from a bordering sidewalk. With the sun shining and all the birds and squirrels, it seemed like quite a pleasant place to call home.

One of the houses along Boulder Street had to belong to Joanie's mother, but I didn't know which one. My eyes followed the sheriff's vehicle until it pulled along the curb, but I lost sight of Anders behinds some shrubs and didn't see which house he approached.

I walked through the park trying to imagine the terror the girl felt as she fled from the billowing black shape with the yellow eyes. My imagination added the teeth I'd seen in my vision, and I shuddered.

I wasn't over the experience of witnessing Kurz's death through his own eyes. Finding a picnic table near the end of the park close to Highway 257, I sat on the top with my feet resting on one of the benches. The sun was high in the sky. It was mid-morning. I still had some time to kill before my lunch date. I remembered Rose's winks and my cheeks flushed again.

My mind raced as I considered the details I'd gleaned as I experienced the horror of Dave Kurz's demise. Would the money have been delivered to Kurz's bank account if he'd followed the rules? I suspected the answer was yes. To do that remotely indicated access to technology and the knowledge of how to use it. Interesting.

The voice that Kurz heard was male. Was this thing some sort of mutated man? A freak of science? Some experiment gone wrong?

Yet, the monster had been locked inside the container. Why? Why would it lock itself inside? What if Kurz had totally forgotten to unlock it? Did it have a secondary exit? A backup plan? And why was the container delivered to this little town? Why was the antique furniture inside the container arranged to make it look like a living space? I had a lot of questions but very few answers.

Was there anything else I could glean from the visions? I leaned back on the table and reviewed the images, horrid as they were. I answered myself out loud. "Yes. Apparently, this thing—whatever it is—doesn't like sunlight." But was it a dislike, or was it something more? I didn't know. "It operates in the shadows, in the darkness."

As I contemplated Kurz's death, the images of my own bloody fate from the previous night's vision returned. *Is what happened to Kurz going to happen to me*? Again, I considered leaving town. Right away. Immediately. I could hitch a ride and get miles away. But would that change my destiny? Would I escape the premonition? Maybe. I might. Then the thought of Joanie fleeing through the park returned.

"I can't leave now," I muttered, "More people are going to die at the teeth of that creature." I couldn't leave. Something inside me demanded I stay; it demanded I face whatever fate was coming. Leaving, as appealing as it was, wasn't an option. There was something deeply embedded in me that forced me to stay put, to take action. "Maybe something in all this information I've gathered can help stop it."

I strode to the sidewalk along the main drag and looked both ways. An old man approached, walking with a cane. He wore a plain blue, short-sleeved, button-down work shirt, blue jeans, and a green cap bearing some agricultural company logo. His hands were gnarled, claw-like, and he was missing the little finger on his right hand. A pouch of chewing tobacco stuck out of his shirt pocket.

"Sir, does this little town have a library?" I asked.

He was a little hunched over, so he sent me a sideways glance, upward past one side of the cap's bill. "Yessir," he answered. His teeth were stained brown. "It's back that way." He motioned to the east. "Past Floyd's Carwash and across from the school." A slight amount of brown drool leaked from the corner of his mouth.

Saying nothing more, he trundled west, toward the general store. I marched east toward the library with sweat droplets forming on my forehead. Maybe a little research would give me some answers.

The Lester Robbins Memorial Library was a huge, solidly built structure formed from giant slabs of limestone. Similar long slabs served as the four steps leading to oak doors hung with iron hardware. The name of the place was chiseled into the stone above the door. I walked inside, cold air slamming me in the face. The AC was running hard. It felt awesome.

Green-shaded reading lamps lit multiple small, rectangular tables scattered around an open center. Skylights overhead provided more pockets of brightness, giving the overall room a dappled look. Two stories of bookshelves lined a middle area filled with tables. A staircase ran upward to my left. A librarian stood behind a counter to my right—an older lady with bluish gray hair. Her reading glasses hung from a flexible cord around her neck, resting on the front of her neatly pressed white blouse. A scent of a floral perfume drifted past my nose carrying with it a hint of tobacco.

"Do you have computers for public use?" I asked with a smile.

"Back corner on the right," she said, her words just above a whisper. She pointed with a long, bony finger. Her red polish seemed to contradict her otherwise quiet demeanor.

Leaving the woman, I weaved through the various tables, their chairs neatly pushed in and arranged symmetrically. I found the computer cubicles in the rear. Bookshelf columns, extending inward from the side and back walls, met in the corner, but they stopped just short, leaving a pseudo-doorway to the electronic devices.

I made my way to a cubicle, the one closest to the

corner, and sat on the hard, oak chair. With my back to the studious room, I fingered the mouse. The screen flashed to life. I found the web browser and clicked the cursor into the search bar.

Now, mind you, I can't tell you how I knew how to do this. I don't remember ever learning about computers and search engines, not to mention a mouse or a keyboard. It was sheer instinct—or maybe something embedded in my brain for a reason. On a basic level, I don't even remember being taught to read or spell words. I know what the word *school* means; I just don't remember ever attending one. How can I forget everything I do and everything that's ever happened to me, but somehow remember language and skills and some social references? It's like someone programmed my brain to constantly self-clean the memory cache but leave all the core details.

Sitting there, I stared at the screen. What exactly I should search for eluded me. What parameters should I set? I decided to input the key points that seemed true: night creature, yellow eyes, large teeth, speaks English. Most of the results were less than helpful. None contained all the search parameters. I read something about sleep paralysis and a creature that mythology said caused it, excerpts from *Frankenstein*, and medical information about yellow teeth.

I scrolled through a few pages and happened upon an obscure news article from something tagged *Weird News Publications*. It had the look of a tabloid, but the title caught my eye.

"Night Creature Stalks Berlin"

The date on the article was a few months prior. It took me ten minutes to read it, and the details matched up well. For two months last winter, people were disappearing, mostly young people out alone at night. They were never recovered. In a few close calls, witnesses claimed it was a dark figure in a billowing, long coat, with large teeth and yellow eyes.

One near-miss victim said the monster pulled her into an alley. It spoke to her in German, laughing about her unfortunate fate. Lucky for her, a group of young men had noticed her being pulled into the shadows from across the street. They rushed to her rescue, but the evil predator escaped. One of the men said it was a vampire. He added that it climbed the walls of the four-story buildings that lined the passageway, leaping from side to side, before disappearing over the top and into the night. A police report discounted his version, claiming he was intoxicated.

"Hmm," I whispered, rubbing my chin. *A vampire?* I picked up two more details from the story. *It can climb like a squirrel, and it can be hurt.* How else could the men have frightened it off?

I punched in a few more combinations of descriptive words. "Monster that avoids light," and "Intelligent night predator with yellow eyes." The results were mostly about old Dracula movies. Nothing truly helpful came up, but I did learn a little about lions that I'll forget by tomorrow.

"Having any luck on your research?"

I nearly jumped out of my skin. The mouse flew out of my hand, and I banged my knees on the table. Whipping around, I found the old librarian lady standing behind me. Her reading glasses sat on her nose as she examined the screen I'd been studying.

"Are you a monster story buff?" she asked. "Personally, I can't stand the genre. I don't see why anyone would fill their minds with that garbage, but who am I to judge? If you like it, it's no skin off my chin. I prefer nonfiction. History and biographies, mostly. Stuff that feeds my brain. Fantasy? Horror? Paranormal? We've got whole sections devoted to that trash. What a waste of paper."

I forced a smile. Some folks judge others and don't even know they're doing it. "It was only a mild curiosity. Truth be told, I'm more a fan of science fiction." I was lying since I had no idea what I liked to read. "I'm about done here, I think. Thanks for offering to help," I added even though she'd done no such thing.

The woman smiled and turned away. She waved over her right shoulder as she headed back to the front desk.

After another ten minutes of exploring information on vampires, I gave up on the web search and glanced toward a clock hanging on one of the few walls not lined with books. The morning was slipping away like cold air through a cracked window, so I decided to shift gears. It was time to investigate the scrapyard and see what the apparition of Jasper Fresno wanted me to find.

Strolling past the front desk, I waved at the silver-haired librarian with the bright nail polish. She watched me over the reading glasses, again on her nose, but otherwise didn't respond. Perhaps the woman was a little gruff, but there was something about her I liked. She reminded me of a grandmother, and it made me wonder if I had a grandma somewhere. "See you next time," I said as I pushed open the main door and ran into a wall of hot air.

The sun was high and the humidity oppressive. I glanced upward as I stood on the front steps and examined the line of the bluff above the trees. The abandoned house sat alone above a wall of sheer rock, staring back like an owl might stare down at a field mouse. There was evil up there; I could literally feel it.

Ten minutes later, after I stopped in front of the General to grab a glimpse of Rose, I stood outside the junkyard where I hooked my fingers through the chain-link fence. My clean clothes were now moist with sweat. My eyes explored the piles of twisted metal. Scrapped vehicles stood in rows with dirt lanes running in between, just wide enough to allow a large forklift to traverse.

I saw no sign of Jasper's ghost. The first gate I came to was locked up tight. The sun reflected off the sharp edges of the razor wire lining the top, reminding me that climbing over wasn't a good idea unless I wanted to slice myself up like human steak, which I didn't. The second gate was a better option. It stood wide open, allowing easy access for any customers looking for used auto parts. I strolled in like I owned the place.

To my left were rows of semi tractors in various states of disassembly and general destruction, twisted and misshapen from highway accidents. To my right were passenger cars in similar conditions. Straight ahead, the rutted dirt drive with a semblance of gravel led toward a small, stone office building. A line of pickup trucks with junk in the beds were queued up, leading toward the left side of that building. My eyes continued to explore the melee as I wandered beyond the waiting vehicles.

An oversized fork truck crossed in front of me, cutting me off. I stopped short, smiled, and waved at the guy driving as if I was his old friend. The man glanced down. He stared at me for a moment, then lifted his radio. After he spoke into the mic, he continued on into the rows to my left.

The cars and trucks were getting older as I worked my way toward the rear. Screeching metal and a large thud drew my attention toward the far back right corner where a massive pressing machine was condensing cars into metal pancakes. Another fork truck was idling nearby, a smashed Toyota rested on its forks. All the metal-on-metal friction had worn the tips of the forks into sharp edges.

To the left of the vehicle press was an enormous pile of tires. The crest of Mount Tread-bare was even with the peak of the roof over the pressing-machine structure. It spread maybe a hundred feet from side to side and fifty feet deep with all makes and sizes from Yokohama to Goodyear, tractor tires to bike tires. Along the bottom edge, weeds were growing through the centers of some. On the left side, small trees had formed a few years of growth through the gaps in the rubber rings.

Jasper Fresno glowed as he sat on one of the tires about midway up the pile. His sad, sparkling eyes met mine, then he glanced between his feet toward the heart of the pile. His right hand pointed downward.

The implication was clear. His remains were somewhere under that pile. Another implication was also true. He didn't end up there by accident. I mean, a guy could accidentally drive off a ravine and be lost in a forested gully. That happens. But nobody leaves an auto-parts store in a neighboring city and inadvertently drives their truck into the center of a pile of tires in a scrapyard. Someone put him there. *Hid* him there.

"Hey, punk. Did you get lost?"

The words reached me despite the noise of the car crusher nearby, and I assumed that I was the punk being addressed. I glanced around anyway just in case there was another punk in the vicinity, but I saw no one else that fit the description.

The voice came from behind me. It was loud and gruff. My imagination formed an image of the guy. Older. Chubby. T-Shirt, soaked in sweat. Crewcut. Crowbar in hand.

When I turned to face my verbal assailant, I got one thing right. He was older. It was his two henchmen, one on each side of him, that were the chubby, T-shirted, crowbar-holding, crewcut-sporting dudes. Well, truth be told, they were more stocky than chubby. Otherwise, the description was accurate. The man behind the voice was maybe sixty, bald, and wore a short-sleeved dress shirt. A pen sprouted from a small pocket on his left chest. I recognized his eyes. Same size, shape, and eyebrows as those on Ronnie's face, the lady-beater from last night. At this point, it was a logical guess based on appearance, but I was reasonably sure that the guy yelling at me was probably Ronnie's dad.

"What're you doing back here, boy? This area's off limits to the public. It's dangerous."

I gathered from the metal rods the bodyguards held that the danger was from more than the industrial equipment. "Following a ghost," I replied. I didn't see a need to lie.

"Are you getting smart with me?"

Perhaps hanging around in the back of a scrapyard with a buried body and two thugs manhandling crowbars wasn't such a good plan. Even though it didn't fit my vision of my own demise from the previous night, I could easily end up hidden under that pile, too. Besides, the two henchmen tapping their respective weapons in their free hands were out of sync, and that bothered me.

"No sir. Sorry, I was just curious. I heard the machine running and wondered what it was." I pointed at the car-crusher. Okay, so I do occasionally tell a fib, but only to avoid being buried under a rubber mountain.

"Only employees are allowed back here," the man said. "Safety reasons. But, no harm, no foul, I suppose."

"Again, I apologize. I meant no harm." I angled my way toward the rutted path leading to the exit.

"Fellas, escort this kid to the gate. Make sure he leaves safely."

The security team flanked me on the way out as I considered the clues. Someone had intentionally placed Fresno's vehicle under that pile of rubber rings, but it was done a long time ago. Clearly the guy I presumed to be Ronnie's dad ran the place. Maybe he owned it. I knew Ronnie was capable of violence, but Jasper Fresno disappeared around three decades ago. Ronnie might have been a twinkle in his dad's eye about then but nothing more. Maybe Ronnie inherited his penchant for violence, though.

The men shoved me through the gate. As I stepped on the berm of the roadway, I glanced back at the piles of mangled steel. Jasper's ghost stood between the guards, looking a tad forlorn, eyes sparkling but sad.

I now knew with one hundred percent certainty where the missing man's truck and his remains could be found. The problem was the lack of proof. I could see Fresno's ghost, but no one else could. I could walk Sheriff Anders to within about thirty feet of the truck, but he wouldn't be able to see under the tires. With a shrug, I said, "I'm sorry," trying to assuage the disappointment evident on the forlorn ghost's face.

"We don't care. Just get on down the road," said the guy on the right as he tapped the heavy rod into his palm.

"I wasn't talking to you," I replied and looked at the apparition flickering between the bullies. Turning away, I trudged my way back toward the General and the cute girl working behind the counter.

Six

Journal Excerpts

How do I know the various details that I know? How do I know how to use a computer when I don't remember ever using one at any other time in my life?

Did someone program me?

In some ways, I feel like an actual computer that's only loaded with random information.

The air-conditioning inside the library was awesome.

The librarian was snoopy and a bit snooty, but I liked her anyway.

I get the sense that I like most people.

The yellow-eyed hunter could very well be a vampire.

The cold air hit me in the face as I stepped inside the convenience store, and after the oppressive heat of the junkyard, it was a welcome relief. Besides the Quarry Pit diner, the little store seemed to be the only other example of commercial success in Cutters Notch, but then again, I hadn't seen the whole town. Rose, with her long curly brown hair, stood behind the counter, laughing, and chatting with a customer. *Forty years old. Ha! There's no way she's forty years old.*

She waved and pointed for me to have a seat at a nearby table. There were three of them lined up along the front windows, benches on either side. I took the closest one, shifting my angle so I could watch her work.

I sat there sensing the psychic messages from her house across the road as they hit the beach of my mind like energy waves. Mixed signals. At times, they seemed to be inviting me over. *Come see us.* The voices of those vibrations in my head seemed plural. Pleasant. At other times, a singular, angry voice tried to dissuade me from visiting. *Stay away from me.* Mind you, these weren't exactly actual voices I was hearing. They were feelings, vibrations, and psychic energy that formed clearly into words. The house had a power that hit me even as I sat in that little store.

Glancing through the window at the gravel drive leading to Rose's house, I wondered what I'd find if I did venture there. It wasn't the structure itself putting out those bands of energy. There was something else there, apparently more than one. Not the yellow-eyed monster, but something.

Pulling my mind away from the paranormal input, I turned my eyes to the merchandise on display nearby. A rotating pedestal stood at the end of the aisle closest to me, stocked with multiple combinations of nuts— some were mixed types, some had bits of chocolate, and some were packaged with raisins. The shelf directly across from me was stocked with automotive materials from motor oil to windshield-wiper fluid. Lacking a car of my own, as far as I knew, I wasn't much interested in that stuff.

I could see Rose clearly from my seat. She was framed by candy bars, beef jerky, and wires for charging cell phones. Her lips turned up in a smile as she worked; her left ear was just visible under her waves of brown hair. I noticed a hint of red in the dark curls, not quite auburn. It was only a hint.

Mesmerized, I had to pull my eyes away. I didn't want her to catch me staring at her. Instead, I watched a guy in gym shorts and flip-flops pumping gas into an old station wagon; an unlit cigarette dangled from his lips.

Eventually, my eyes lost focus as my mind began to work on the problem of how to arrange for Jasper Fresno's remains to be found. Although I knew he was under the tires, how could I convince others that he was there? How would I get him out? Those were the questions for which I needed answers.

I replayed the images of the junkyard and the piled tires, the goons with the crowbars, and the guy running the show. The gate to the complex was across the road from the Quarry Pit diner. The Sheriff's Office was maybe a quarter mile closer to town. My quandary was how to convince the sheriff to look under the tires. To do it officially, he'd need a warrant and he'd need probable cause to get that. He could ask permission, but since old Fresno was likely hidden there on purpose, I doubted anyone working there would grant it.

The sheriff wouldn't even investigate the apparently vacant old house on the bluff without a warrant, and let's face it, the word of a drifter kid who claimed to have seen a ghost wasn't exactly compelling evidence. It was a pickle, a quandary, a perplexing puzzle, but there had to be a solution.

"There must be a way I can get him to dig into that pile without a warrant," I mumbled to myself.

"Get who to look into what pile?" It was Rose.

Suddenly, she was standing directly beside my table. I hadn't seen her approach. I jerked, jumping to my feet in surprise.

"Sorry, Doc. Didn't mean to scare you."

After forcing my heart back into my chest, I sat back down and chuckled. "Whoa, yeah. I was off in another world trying to work out a predicament." I took a deep breath. Several breaths.

"Let's go have some lunch, and you can tell me all about it," Rose said. "I've got a whole hour until I need to be back." A middle-aged man sporting a greasy-haired ponytail was now working behind the counter. I'd been so deep into the Fresno problem that I didn't even see him come in.

"Where're we going? Quarry Pit?"

"Nope." She pointed across the highway. "My place. Just over there. I bet you forgot where I live, right?"

"No. Actually, it's sort of ingrained in my memory now."

"If that's true, you're truly a unique individual."

She led the way, and I followed her out the door, trying not to stare at her shape as she walked. I failed. Rose had a curvy figure that moved nicely with her every step. I closed the gap between us, forcing my mind to behave.

She led me diagonally across the lot, beyond the gas pumps to the sidewalk. We didn't go to the intersection but were angling directly for her driveway. As we stood there watching the traffic and looking for an opening to cross, the positive and negative vibes from her house were still assaulting my brain. With the cars still flowing through the green light at Robbins Creek Road, I closed my eyes and tried to force the psychic tremors into submission. Flashes of color shimmered behind my eyelids. This was going to be an interesting lunch—I had no doubt.

"Hey, Moon-boy! I'm still gonna get you."

I opened my eyes to see traffic stopping at the crossroad and a souped-up classic Chevy Camaro hot rod rumbling near the back of the line. It was dark blue with lots of chrome. The wheels were oversized, raising the rear end higher than the original design intended. Ronnie was hanging half out the driver's side window, assaulting me with a sneer. "In fact, let's do this right now," he added. "I'm gonna kick your ass."

"Come on," Rose interjected. "He won't follow us far." She grabbed my elbow and pulled me into the road, dragging me across the pavement. Rose glared at Ronnie over her shoulder. "He's such a piece of work these days."

Ronnie jerked the steering wheel, gunned the engine, and pulled his car into the opposing lane, squealing the tires. Smoke rose from his Goodyears as he looped into the General's lot. We reached the opposite side of the road as he jumped from his front seat to pursue us, crowbar in hand. *What is it with crowbars in this town?*

The town bully was already halfway across Highway 257 as Rose and I stepped into her driveway.

Rose stopped short and turned to watch as Ronnie approached. "Watch this," she said whispering into my ear. Her breath was warm on my skin but still sent a tickling shiver down my back. "Just don't say anything."

We were standing on her driveway in what I thought was plain sight, right at the entrance from the road. I tried to push Rose behind me as I took up a defensive stance, ready to defend both of us, my instincts indicating that I could deal with this guy.

My nemesis with the metal bar stopped right in front of us and scanned both ways, a look of confusion painting his face. "Where'd you go, Moon-boy?" His brow was furrowed, and his eyes were squinting as they darted from side to side. Sweat beads formed on his temples and ran down through his scruffy whiskers.

Rose and I were nearly nose to nose with him, but Ronnie couldn't see us. She raised her index finger to her lips, urging me to stay quiet. More sweat glistened on his forehead and soaked through the armpits of his work shirt. I could see the words "Castle Scrapyard" stenciled on the right chest; "Ronnie" was stenciled on the left.

So, he worked at the junkyard. The shirt reinforced my impression that the guy in charge of the piles of twisted metal—and the pile of tires—was his dad. Standing this close in the light of day, the resemblance was remarkable.

Ronnie paced to the right, then back to the left, finally stopping directly in front of us again. We were standing there with the sun striking our faces, and he couldn't see us.

"You can hide, but I'll eventually find you," Ronnie finally said. Then he growled, actually growled, before returning to his still-rumbling car. After he jumped in and slammed the door, Rose tugged my elbow to lead me up her driveway.

"It's the house," she explained. "It blocks people's minds somehow. If it doesn't want you to come near, you won't even be able to see the driveway. That's why no one can ever remember where I live. It's also why it's so unusual that you can."

"Why's it letting me in?" My hands were still shaking from the confrontation with Ronnie. I crossed my arms to hold them still. "Why can I see it and remember it?"

"I don't know. Your ability to see through the veil is a first for me. I've lived here for years now, and it's never happened before…except once, a long time ago and that was a very different situation." She paused and smiled; her eyes drifted as she apparently thought back across the years. "I noticed the blocking effect right after I moved in. People could never remember my address. I'd invite them over and they'd forget. At first, it made me a bit insecure. I thought people were ignoring me. When I realized it was the house, it gave me a sense of security. I didn't have to worry about some creep following me home from work. These days, it leaves me feeling isolated and lonely. I even have to pick up my mail at the post office because the mailman doesn't realize there's a house here."

It was definitely going to be an interesting lunch.

"I should have expected that it might eventually happen, though. I never noticed the house myself until the woman who owned it before me asked me to come help her with some chores. Then, everything changed." Rose paused and glanced back over her shoulder. "I was a teenager sitting at a picnic table that used to be right outside the General. Minerva Woodstock walked over, sat with me, and suddenly I could see the driveway."

Rose turned back toward the house. She and I walked side by side, our hands almost touching. I could feel a tingle in my fingers, the anticipation of a touch that didn't happen.

"You know, Ronnie wasn't always such a creep. He was a pretty sweet kid when he was little. Cute little blond boy. His whole world was turned upside down when his mother died."

"He's an orphan?"

"His dad raised him. Just the two of them, but his dad worked most of the time, leaving Ronnie to fend for himself and deal with his grief on his own. I've literally watched the boy change before my eyes over the last ten years."

A tinge of sympathy sprang to life in my heart. I guess even a bully has a backstory. "Did you go to school with him?" I still wasn't buying the whole *Rose is forty-years-old* thing.

She gave me a glance and smiled. "You're so sweet." Rose looped her hand through the crook of my elbow as we walked, causing a surge of blood to hit my face. Still, she didn't answer the question.

As we strolled to the house through the huge trees and along the winding gravel driveway, I was amazed by the immense limestone wall that rushed upward behind the Victorian structure. There was no back way in or out, and the forest was thick all around.

Rose didn't use her front door. It was solid wood with a large pane of ornate glass in the upper half— stained around the outer edge leaving a clear oval in the center. I could see a lamp on a table just inside. Rather, we continued to follow the drive around the right side of the structure. I admired the intricate wood trim. Each feature was wrapped in interwoven, hand-placed wooden decoration. It was truly beautiful, even if it did need a coat of paint.

Eventually, we found ourselves at a simple back door—hardwood also, with a rectangular pane of clear glass. It had an antique knob but a more modern deadbolt lock. I wondered why she even needed a lock if the house made itself invisible to outsiders. Rose must have wondered the same thing because she didn't have the house locked, despite the mechanism. She simply turned the knob and opened the door.

I was struck again when we stepped inside—not with amazement but with a surge of power. It was as if I dove into a pool of cold water that was hiding a downed powerline. The rush of psychic energy nearly knocked me over. I stumbled in the mudroom and would have fallen down Rose's basement stairs if she hadn't grabbed my arm.

"Whoa," I said, my head spinning. Eventually, I gathered myself as Rose guided me to a kitchen chair. "This place is an ocean of paranormal power."

"Really? Can you see it or just feel it?" she asked as she filled a glass with water at the sink. I didn't answer right away, so she placed the drink in front of me, then took a seat on the opposite side of the table. "Obviously, I know there's power here, and I can sense presences, but I never see anything."

Then something else happened that you don't see every day. Well, maybe I do, and I simply don't remember. Three ghosts wandered into the room—a small, smiling girl wearing a simple dress; an old, scowling woman with her hair pulled back in a bun; and a balding, middle-aged man. The man glared at me. They formed a luminescent line, peering at me from over Rose's shoulders. I could see others wandering around inside the adjoining dining room, mostly teenage girls, but a few boys, too. They gathered up behind the trio in front, all peering in with unblinking eyes. There were dozens. I lost count.

"I can definitely see it," I finally said. "Them, actually. Ghosts. Dozens of ghosts."

"Are they right here in the room with us?" Rose glanced around. "Do they look like real people or more like apparitions?" Her lower lip was quivering.

"Some are in here; there are three in front, and the others are backed up into the other room behind them."

"You can really see them that clearly?"

"I can. Absolutely. The three in front are a young girl, an old woman with a hair bun, and a balding middle-aged man. The girl seems friendly, welcoming. The other two, not so much. They seem angry. Those three seem to be the leaders. The others are standing very still just behind them."

Rose contemplated what I said for a moment or two. "Hmm." She stood, pulled a loaf of bread from atop the refrigerator, and retrieved some containers from inside the appliance. Now that I described them, she didn't seem particularly concerned about our spectral lunch companions. Besides the little lip quiver, she shrugged off the information like old news. She pulled plates from a cabinet and retrieved a couple of sodas. After getting some ice from the freezer, she placed our lunch on the table.

All the while, the ghosts looked on. The old woman and the balding man glared, but the rest of the crew simply observed; a few smiled. The little spectral girl wandered over and took up a spot at my left arm. She leaned this way and that, examining me. It was unnerving, but I didn't feel threatened.

Rose pointed at the plate in front of me with a large ham-and-turkey sandwich, some potato salad, and a small bowl of fresh fruit. The sandwich was piled high with a couple different types of cheeses, lettuce, tomato, and pickled jalapeños. "Do you like ham and turkey together?"

"Beats me," I replied. "Let's find out."

We ate in silence with an equally silent audience. The sandwich was delicious, the jalapeños adding just the right pop of flavor.

"You believed me when I told you about the ghosts, right?" I eventually asked. I was beginning to wonder if maybe she thought I was crazy. Or maybe I was wondering about my own sanity and was looking for a little validation.

"Sure." She smiled and took another bite.

"You're not alarmed?"

"No."

"Do you know who they are?"

"Yes."

The old woman ghost with the hair bun moved up behind Rose, then glared down at the top of my host's head. The balding guy joined her.

"You know who all of them are? There must be three dozen different apparitions here. There's at least thirty. How do you know them all?" I was starting to wonder if it was a good idea for me to be alone with Rose in this house, especially if no one in the area even remembered the house was here. No one would have been able to see us enter the driveway. Maybe she was a spider, and I was her prey. Maybe the thing with the yellow eyes and sharp teeth wasn't the only monster in town.

Rose was still gazing down at her food when she added, "I've done my homework."

The eyes of the angry old woman flared in their sockets as the ghost leaned over Rose's shoulder. With a horrid, snarling look, she stuck her hands into my host's head, all the way in until her thumbs were pressing against Rose's freckled forehead.

Rose jerked upright—eyes wide, palms flat on the table. "She murdered us!" The voice boomed out of Rose's mouth, then it echoed back from other parts of the house. "She killed us right here in my home."

I decided lunch was over and I should leave.

As I stood, the ghost of the little girl slammed into the old woman, knocking the apparition away with such force that it passed through the wall and out of sight. Then she, in turn, placed her hands inside Rose's head, a little less violently.

Calming my heart with a deep breath, I sat back down.

"She lies," indicating the apparition she'd flung away. "She was the murderer. I should know, being her first victim, accident or not." As if she'd read my thoughts, the girl added, "Minerva was my sister. She used to lure young ones here like a spider lures a fly. She killed them to steal their youth like she stole mine. My death was an accident. The rest were not."

Despite the explanation, I still thought leaving was one of my better ideas. I'd just stand up, walk back out the rear door, make my way to the highway, and then keep on walking right out of Cutters Notch. Fresno had waited this long; he could keep waiting. I sure didn't need any more encounters with brain-invading ghosts or a run-in with a monster baring a mouth full of teeth.

Gently, the girl removed her grip on Rose's mind. My host gasped and came back to herself. "What happened?" Her eyes were as wide as half-dollar coins. Sweat beads gathered on her temples where the spectral hands had entered her brain.

The ghosts wandered off. The bald male apparition hung around for a few moments, then followed the others out of the room. I guessed the show was over and took another deep breath.

"They used you as a puppet. Spoke right out of your mouth. I don't remember if I've ever gone to a horror movie, but that was some freaky, scary stuff right there."

"What did they say?" Rose leaned over the table toward me.

"The old woman said you murdered her, but the young girl defended you, claiming the old woman had been the murderer. That's about it." After a moment, I added "I'm not an exorcist." I paused and considered the black hole that was my past. "At least I don't think I am. I don't have a clue how to help you with this." Nothing in my embedded instincts provided me any insight. "But I will say this, the child is the most powerful of the ghosts. She's the strongest by far. The old woman and the baldheaded ghost are dangerous, though. This is not a good place to live. If I were you, I'd move."

"I've thought about moving a lot." She turned and stared at the window above the sink. "I can't seem to bring myself to go. Every time I start to consider the idea, something changes my mind."

Understanding exactly how that could happen, I stood again. I decided I'd best leave before some apparition stuck its hands inside my brain. "Rose, thank you for lunch. It was tasty and more interesting than I even anticipated. I've got some things to do, and I'm pretty sure you have an afternoon shift to work."

My host stood with me; the shape of her figure captured my attention as she rose. Somehow, I managed to shift my eyes to her face. Her eyes locked onto mine, and I stared at her lips as she spoke. "We never discussed your predicament, remember? Something about getting someone to dig into a pile of something, right?"

Tearing my mind away from my growing infatuation, I tried hard to focus on her words. "Yeah, I'm still working that out, but it's nothing you need to worry about. It's not your problem."

All at once, out of the blue, Rose grabbed me and pulled me into a hug, wrapping both arms around me and squeezing as if I were in a human hydraulic press. She was warm and soft. Endorphins shot through me. Just as quickly, and to my disappointment, she released me.

"I'm sorry," she said, dropping her eyes to the floor. "It's just that it means a lot to me to know it's not all in my head. I'm not crazy." She smiled and pulled a brown, curly lock of hair back from her cheek. "Oh, I'm quirky, for sure. Always have been. But you've reassured me that I'm not completely bonkers."

Still lost in the hug, I barely heard her words. All my senses were on fire. She didn't need her ghosts to stick their hands in my brain. She'd already snagged it with the press of her body against mine, soft in some places, harder in others. I knew I'd never get her out of my mind—at least not for the next twenty-four hours.

"And you make me feel seen," she added. "Others see me for a moment and then forget me, but you see me. You really see me. Guess I miss that more than I knew."

The ghosts began to reenter the room, starting with the main three, as if to counterbalance the hug with the fact they could stick their hands in her head and make her talk. The old woman and the balding man bore scowling countenances. That brought me back down from wherever it was my mind had floated.

"I have to be back at the store in a few minutes," Rose said. "Maybe we could talk some more after I get off work?" She grinned. I had the distinct impression that she had something more in mind. As enticing as that idea was, the brain-invading ghosts were a real buzz kill, and I was still weighing the idea of fleeing town altogether.

———•●•———

I stepped out of Rose's driveway and onto the sidewalk that stretched along the main road through the strange little town. It was palpable when I felt the supernatural power of the ghosts release their hold on me. I was visible again. The whole experience had been surreal. Even so, I decided not to leave town—not yet anyway.

Glancing at the sun, I saw it was still high in the sky. Lots of daylight left. Lots of time before that thing with the yellow eyes, whatever it is, would emerge again with the sunset. I still had time to make a difference.

There wasn't much I could do to help Rose, but at

least I'd told her what she was up against. I still felt the pressure of two other matters clawing at my mind—one was the old mystery of what happened to Jasper Fresno, and one was the newer danger posed by the creature from the house on the bluff.

I still hadn't figured out how to convince the cops to dig into that pile of tires, but just as I'd thought in Rose's kitchen, Jasper had waited this long; he could wait a while longer. The other matter was a different story. That one had a deadline of sunset, not to mention my own potential deadline a couple of hours later. Three young people close to my own age had gone missing in the last three weeks. Maybe they were dead. Probably they were dead. But maybe they were still alive. It was going to be a good, long walk, but I decided to revisit that abandoned house overlooking Cutters Notch.

Seven

Journal Excerpts

There is no way that Rose is forty years old. I don't believe it.

Rose's house has a strange power. It seems to block everyone from seeing it or even being aware of its existence...except for me. It has granted me access.

I can see a lot of ghosts. Some of them are very angry.

Rose makes a tasty lunch. She likes me because I can "see" her.

———• ● •———

I was thirsty and sweating when I reached the gate blocking the driveway to the once majestic structure. Climbing the winding road leading to the top of the bluff was not an easy stroll. It was steeper than it seemed when I rode in the sheriff's car. Each switchback was marked with large, square, limestone blocks camouflaged by overgrown shrubbery. There were more of the cut stones than I'd noticed on my drive up with the sheriff. It wouldn't be safe to come down that hill on an icy day.

A bottle of water would've come in handy, but I

hadn't considered that as I passed the little store. I was on a mission I hadn't fully thought through, so I headed uphill with nothing to drink.

I found myself out of breath with salty water running off my face like a leaky faucet as I gripped the vertical metal rungs in the hinged gate. The sun was still high overhead but starting its trek toward the western horizon, reminding me that I had a deadline.

The road was deserted. Only a couple of cars passed me as I made the long hike up, and not one of them stopped to offer me a ride. I felt very alone, very vulnerable, like I could just disappear, and no one would know I was gone. In my case, I suppose that was true. I'd drifted into town; they'd assume I drifted out. Gator and Rose might wonder about me, but that would pass quickly enough. Something could happen to me, and there'd be no one to miss me.

Across the road from the house behind an industrial chain-link fence, there was a gray emptiness. Even the forest was gone. A deserted industrial site overrun with scrub brush was the only sign that civilization had once been there. No other homes in sight. A rusty sign dangled on the fence: "Robbin's Stone." Scattered around the lot were old barrels, a few block buildings, and a couple dilapidated conveyors. A crow perched on a red, wheelless Ford flatbed truck, which was itself resting on wooden blocks.

The vacant area seemed like a logical place for a monster to hide. There had to be dozens of creepy cracks and crevices for the thing to lurk inside. Maybe it wasn't still in the garage behind me anymore. Maybe it was over there in one of the vacant industrial buildings. I could feel the evil presence, but I wasn't sure of the direction from which the sense was flowing.

I scaled the rusty fence around the industrial site and dropped on the other side, landing on an old concrete pad. The surface of the lot was broken in many places with weeds, grass, and even small trees sprouting through the openings. A grasshopper leapt at my face; I swatted and ducked.

Most of the buildings were boarded up around the base but with missing chunks of roof and open skylights. Others were wide open with broken windows and missing doors. Not good places for a creature that hates sunlight. There was one building, however, that looked promising. The windows were boarded, the roof was intact, and the doors were closed up tight.

Circling the structure, I investigated, checking for other points of entry. No vibes, good or bad, emanated from the place. The windows were sealed, and the doors were all padlocked and seemed undisturbed in the last several years, maybe decades. Whatever creatures lurked inside were probably hairy and very small.

The vacant Victorian house across the road, sitting on the edge of the bluff with its nearby oversized garage was, however, putting out vibes—dark, ominous vibes. From where I stood in the shade of the leafy branches of a tree-of-heaven, I could now feel the vibes clearly flowing from the dilapidated estate. The old mansion seemed to be staring at me, daring me to come in for a look-see.

"That thing's in there. I can feel it." No one heard me but the crow. It squawked in response, taking flight before I made my move. "Caw, caw," it warned as it circled my position.

The monster's presence was palpable now. It wasn't sleeping anymore. It was awake and aware. I was probing it with my mind, and it was probing me back. I sensed its curiosity.

After climbing back over the chain-link fence, I returned to the locked gate of the Victorian house. Nervousness squiggled in my lower abdomen like a box of nightcrawlers. Despite my trepidation, I scaled the gate and lowered myself to the crushed gravel driveway on the other side. My heart was racing, pounding on my ribcage as if it wanted out.

"What am I doing here?" I asked myself. "I should just leave this crazy little town."

Somehow, I couldn't do it. I couldn't walk away knowing there was a creature here that would keep on killing. Something deep inside was driving me to take action. Whatever was the source of my internal drive, it kept my feet moving forward despite my apprehension.

I took a step, and the bright sunshine disappeared. The day turned dark, enhancing my fear. Looking up, I saw one lonely puff of cloud drifting across the sky, briefly blocking the sun. I paused, waiting for it to pass because I was pretty sure I needed all the daylight I could get.

My footsteps crunched on the tiny, compacted stones as I followed the winding driveway that led past the front porch toward the oversized garage. The windows of the house along the front wall stared back at me as I studied its structure. Limestone walls draped with ivy supported two full stories plus an attic. Ornate woodwork with layers of chipped paint lined the porch roof that spanned the entire width of the building.

After peeking around the corner to the rear of the property, I retraced my way to the porch and climbed the steps. The doors were French-style, double-wide and made of darkly stained wood—oak, no doubt—with stained glass panels. On the doors were two matching brass knockers, one beneath each of the ornate windows. They were shaped like growling dogs.

My hand reached out and gripped the knob even as waves of trepidation again swept through my chest. I thought for sure it would be locked, but the latch clicked, and the mechanism popped free. The hinges creaked when the door swung wide leaving a dark hole that felt like a portal to death. "What am I doing? This is crazy." I wanted to run away, but I couldn't. "Don't go in there," I whispered, then stepped inside anyway.

Dark burgundy draperies covered the windows of the empty rooms. Dust drifted in waves across the floor, bunching up in the corners and along the baseboards. Silky strands, old and new, traversed the space, littered with more dust particles picked up in the air. I saw no footprints on the soiled floorboards. If anyone had recently passed through the space, they had done it without walking, but I couldn't rule out other modes of passage. Maybe vampires can fly.

Of course, the creature could still be hiding out in the shipping container, but why live in a cold metal box when a perfectly terrifying old house was right here? *If I were a monster, where would I be hiding? Basement or attic?* It had to be one of the two. The thing hated daylight, so the basement seemed the more logical choice. I decided attics were for ghosts. Closets and basements were for monsters.

Flailing my arms to keep the wild webs out of my face, I wandered down a bleak hallway toward the rear of the house. I looked back and saw my footprints clearly. The floors creaked no matter how slowly or lightly I stepped. "So much for keeping my presence a secret."

The backdoor had four clear, rectangular panes of glass and looked out over the cliff at the expanse of the forest beyond Cutters Notch. I paused a moment to gather my nerve as I watched that little puff of cloud rushing off into the distance of the southeastern sky. Then, I turned around and peered into what was almost certainly a portal to Hell. An ebony pit where no light escaped. The basement.

The switch on the wall had no effect when I

snapped it up and down. Of course not, there wouldn't be any power running to this old, abandoned mansion. It was then I realized another weakness in my plan—I had no flashlight. Even if that thing was down there, I wouldn't be able to see it. And, it would likely see me clearly, my body heat glowing like the little skin-covered bottle of warm blood that I was.

No matter. I was going down anyway. I had to. Step one—creak. Step two—crack. I turned and put my back to the sidewall. Step three—creak. Pausing, I reached out with my mind into the dark pit below me, probing for what I believed to be a vampire. The dark vibe of the property told me it was close, but I couldn't sense where exactly it was hiding out. It could be down there, or it could be behind me. Regardless, I had to keep going.

I ducked at step four, bending over to pass under a low-hanging ceiling and peer out into what I imagined to be open space below the floor line. Squinting, I worked hard to see into the pit. My muscles tensed like coiled springs in anticipation of anything that might move. I leaned forward, hand on the short wall above my head for support, searching for something, anything. At the same time, I was terrified I'd actually see something—something with big teeth and glaring yellow eyes.

"Hey! Where're you going?"

The voice from behind me ripped any semblance of control I'd managed to contain. I jumped, hit my head on the low ceiling, and tumbled to the bottom of the stairs, landing hard on the concrete floor. Something squeaked and scurried away.

"Doc, you alright?"

Lying on the floor in a lump, I glared up into the beam of a flashlight. A form stood between the artificial torch and the naturally illuminated windowpanes. "That hurt, and you scared the crap outta me," I said.

"What the hell are you doing in here?" Gator asked. The light from his Maglite reflected off the walls and illuminated his face.

"You wouldn't believe me if I told you."

"You might be surprised by what I'd believe. Do you need help up?" He hurried down the steps.

"No. I'm good," I said, waving him off. Being stubborn, I struggled up on my own. Before I could climb the stairs, though, I collapsed as another vision wrapped its tentacles around my brain and squeezed.

My mind's eye swirled amid a million shining stars like a white, sparkling whirlwind. When it dissipated, I found myself feeling disoriented inside a metal chamber. Candles flickered from various points in the rectangular room—one in each corner and a large one on a table before me. They cast undulating shadows on the corrugated walls.

The vampire sat in a large, ornate wooden chair on the other side of the table. It wore a long, dark coat despite the heat. Unblinking yellow eyes stared at me from beneath an oversized hood. Clawed fingers gripped the ends of the chair's armrests, nails like daggers digging into the wood. The gray skin of its hands was so translucent that I could see its bones stretching down each finger.

"I know you are snooping around nearby, searching for me," it said with an accent that was more French than Eastern European. The voice was male, deep, and resonant. It stood.

My gaze turned upward because the creature was much taller than me. It had the form of a man as it stepped around the end of the table. In some ways, the monster felt like a man, human, but alongside and overriding that faint humanity rumbled what I sensed to be a hateful, predatory animal bent on terrorizing its prey.

"Unfortunately," it continued, "with the sun still overhead, I cannot properly greet you. However, there is no need for you to search for me any longer." His use of language forced me to focus on his slight human nature, to see him as more than a dangerous creature.

He paused at an ancient record player, moving the needle to the rotating turntable. Music arose. Bob Seger singing *Night Moves*.

"You see, you have piqued my interest. Soon, the lantern in the sky will sink below the horizon, and I will find you. Oh yes, I will seek you out. You won't be able to hide. Then, we will make proper introductions—oh, yes—proper and personal introductions."

Raising his long, claw-like fingers, he pulled back his hood to reveal his gray-skinned face. The yellow eyes were joined by teeth—two aligned rows of jagged, sharp points protruding from a mouth that stretched from one ear to the other.

He grinned.

I screamed.

———— • ● • ————

I was still screaming when I awoke from the nightmarish daydream. Above me was a very large sugar maple. In front of me, Gator's face was two inches from mine as he pinned my shoulders against the tree. He backed off when he saw my eyes focus on his own. How had I gotten out of that basement and into the shade of the tree?

"You okay now?" he asked. Gator rubbed his back. He must have carried me up.

I didn't answer. Instead, I scrambled to my feet, twisting my head around to get my bearings. We were in the front yard facing the abandoned house. The huge garage was off to my left.

My brain felt scrambled. It was disorienting to be jumping between various realities.

I could feel the creature's presence now. It throbbed at me, pulling at my psyche from the direction of the garage. The vivid images from the dream remained in my conscious mind. The vampire lived in that storage container, if one could call it living, and that container was behind the closed garage doors fifty feet from where Gator and I stood.

"I need to leave town," I announced. Even as I said it, I knew it was useless. Even if I hitched a ride, I'd never be out of that monster's reach. It had marked me. It told me I couldn't hide. It would find me.

Gator had backed away as I scrambled to my feet. Now, he stepped toward me again, placing his hands on my shoulders. "Doc, what's wrong? You look as pale as a bleached-out t-shirt."

Focusing on the deputy's eyes, I pointed toward the outbuilding. "He's in there. Right there."

"Who is?" He glanced at the garage and then back to my eyes.

"The one who's taking your people. He's not a person. Not exactly. Maybe he was at one time. Now, he's not. He…he…he's some sort of creature. A thing that only comes out at night. He's all teeth and yellow eyes."

"What? Like a vampire?"

I glanced at the sky. "Yes, that's it. He's an honest-to-God vampire. The days are long right now, and the sun is still high. He's vulnerable during the day.

We still have time."

"Time for what?"

"We need to move now. Today. Before it gets dark. We need backup, more deputies, more weapons." I strode toward the garage. "He's not just a common criminal, a killer; he's much more than that. He's a monster, an actual monster," I added as I grabbed a handle fastened to one of the large doors.

"Hang on, now." Gator stood back, giving me space.

Unlike the house, the garage was secure, seemingly locked from the inside. I yanked at the large doors, tried the man-door. Nothing would open. "We're going to need something to break open this door."

"Slow down. Take a breath and explain things more fully."

It was my turn to grab Gator's shoulders. I stared him in the eyes. We were standing directly in front of the garage, maybe ten or twenty feet from a monster behind two sets of doors, one wood and the other corrugated metal.

"There is a vampire holed up in that building right there." I said, pointing toward the locked doors. "The monster only comes out at night. He was delivered here on Dave Kurz's truck. Dave was his first victim in Cutters Notch. He got the others who've gone missing since, and he almost snatched Joanie last night. His cover is blown now. He knows that I know he's here. If we don't get him before dark, Cutters Notch will be a bloody mess by tomorrow morning. We'll all be dead." Somehow, I knew this to be true.

• ● •

Ten minutes later, I was sitting in the sheriff's

office, staring at my feet, waiting for Rick Anders to arrive. With shaky hands I took a sip from a new, cold bottle of water. Some missed my mouth and slopped down the front of my shirt.

"Hey, Doc," Anders said as he strode in, carrying a piece of paper. As he walked by, I eyed his service pistol. *Would bullets actually stop a vampire?* "Gator has filled me in on your theory. You have to admit it's a pretty wild story." He chuckled as he sat down and leaned back in his chair. It creaked under the load of his large frame. "That said, it may not be the wildest tale ever told in these parts."

"It's not a theory, and it's not a tale," I replied. "I've seen him…it…whatever it is." I tapped the side of my head.

"One of your visions?"

I nodded. "More than that, though." I told him about the article I'd read at the library, hoping to provide some corroboration.

The sheriff was quiet for a few minutes. He turned slightly and stared out the window as he scratched the close-cropped hair on his head. I let him think, but it seemed like time was speeding toward sundown. Eventually, he turned back to me.

"Look, Doc, I know your journal indicates that you've had some unique experiences. Maybe you have some abilities that are extraordinary, but you need to understand; I have no proof either way. For some reason maybe only God knows, I trust your honesty. Still, it's a huge stretch to connect that tabloid story from Europe to what's going on here in southern Indiana. And I have no probable cause to break into that garage. There's no proof but these visions you've described. I need tangible evidence to get the search warrant. At the minimum, I need some probable cause. Fourth Amendment—I can't simply break in there on the word—or visions—of a young drifter we just met this morning. If you're wrong, there could be hell to pay."

Anxiety rose in my chest. I had to convince him to move on the creature before it got dark. Standing, I paced in front of Anders' desk, burning off some nervous energy. "There'll be hell to pay if I'm right and you don't go in," I replied. "Gator entered the house without a warrant," I reasoned. "Why could he do that, but you can't go in the garage?"

"He was cruising by and saw you go in the house. It gave him probable cause to investigate. Technically, I could charge you with trespassing."

"Sheriff, I'm telling you, that thing is absolutely in there waiting for the sun to set. The way I see it, if you don't go after it now with the sun at your back, it'll be coming out tonight to wreak havoc in this little town. It said it's coming after me, but with its cover blown, all bets are off. People will die. Maybe lots of people. Then, in the aftermath, tomorrow morning, another flatbed truck will show up to carry it away, leaving you—if you're still alive—to clean up the mess."

I could see Anders processing what I'd said. He was looking past me into the void of a dark corner. Wrinkles crossed his forehead. His right hand fidgeted with an ink pen, spinning it around and through his fingers.

"I can't do it," he finally said. "I want to, but I just can't. Not on the basis of visions alone. I'll send Gator back up there to snoop around. If he can find anything concrete, anything I can use for a warrant, we'll go in."

"Sheriff, you're not dealing with a common criminal here. It's a real-life vampire. And it's smart, too. Cunning. Intelligent."

He shook his head and grimaced. "I have to follow the law. If we can't find a verifiable reason to make entry, we'll just need to be extra vigilant tonight. I've known you for what—six or seven hours? I can't move on your claim of visions without appropriate, verifiable evidence to back up what you say."

I paused my pacing to examine the items on his desk. There were two black wire-mesh baskets with various official papers, a coffee cup with an Indianapolis Colts insignia doubling as a penholder, and a tray of paperclips. On one outer corner was a picture frame. Inside its gold metal edges posed a smiling boy in a baseball uniform. Ornate, metal letters spelled a single word on the base of the frame: SON. Sitting on a small pedestal next to the picture was a baseball. "*I love you dad*!" was handprinted in black ink on the scuffed leather.

"Was that your boy's ball?" I asked. Concentrating on the baseball, I could feel the sheriff's attachment to the orb; it was coming off him in waves. It was incredibly special to him. Something he held dear. "Did he give it to you?" I probed, even though I already sensed the answer.

"Yes." A weak smile formed on his lips; a look of melancholy filled his eyes.

I reached for the ball.

"DON'T!" Anders shouted.

Stopping short, I peered at him. His face was red; his eyes flooded with tears. Clearly, the baseball touched a stream of emotion that constantly flowed just beneath the surface of the sheriff's otherwise controlled demeanor.

After taking a breath, he continued, "My son gave it to me last summer. He lived with my first wife in Indianapolis, so I didn't get to see him as much as I would have liked. He was a pitcher for his high school team. They won the state title, and he'd struck out twelve batters. A week later he died in a freak boating accident." Anders swiped the back of his hand across his face to clear the tears. Then he reached out and lightly ran his finger over the seam of the baseball.

"I'm so sorry," I told him. Then I stepped away to a window that gave a view of the back side of the local post office. I could see Highway 257 beyond the northwestern corner of the postal building and the high metal fence around the junkyard beyond that. Jasper Fresno's ghost was peering at me through the chain-link wires.

"It's okay," Anders said. "I overreacted. The loss is still raw, and I've attached my heart to that one souvenir." He picked it up and examined it, or more likely looked through it to a memory he cherished. After a few moments, he replaced it, shifting it so the printing was clearly visible.

A flurry of thoughts raced through my mind as I tried desperately to come up with some way to convince the sheriff that he had no choice but to break into that garage—now, or at least before sundown. The various day's events rushed before my eyes. Yellow eyes and jagged teeth. Ghostly hands slipping into the side of Rose's head. A baseball. Then, Jasper Fresno's sad face appeared right before my nose. *Was I having a panic attack?*

I squeezed my eyes shut, trying to lock out the rushing images, but that did nothing but give them a dark background to shine upon. Teeth. Ghosts. Yellow eyes. Rose. Fresno. Tires. A shipping container. A garage. More teeth. Yellow eyes again, glowing in the dark. A baseball.

I gazed again through the window. Jasper was still shimmering in the afternoon sun. He wasn't going anywhere, stuck as he was beneath that pile of old tires. Turning back, I watched Anders wipe his eyes once more. Then my own eyes fell on the special baseball sitting safely in its spot on the corner of his desk. *He'd do anything to protect that baseball. Anything.*

"I'm sorry for snapping at you," the sheriff said.

I hated doing what I did, but an idea struck me. I was desperate and desperation can drive desperate acts. I wasn't sure the man would ever forgive me. I wasn't sure I'd forgive myself. "I'm sorry, too," I said.

"No need to be." Anders managed a weak smile.

"Yes, there is," I said, fixing my eyes on his. "I am so sorry for this." I snatched up the baseball and sprinted out of his office, slamming the door behind me.

Eight
Journal Excerpts

I really ought to flee this crazy little town. The yellow-eyed evil is aware of me.

The monster is still in the shipping container locked in the mansion's garage,

but the sheriff won't go after it without a warrant.

I must convince him to do it before it gets dark.

I hated doing what I had to do. Desperation drove me.

—— • ● • ——

I could check back through my journal, but I don't think I'm usually a cruel person. That is, I don't feel an urge to hurt others to entertain myself. I can't imagine myself being that middle-school bully on the playground knocking around the new kid for kicks, stealing his lunch money, or rubbing his face in toilet water. Still, what I did to Sheriff Rick Anders was no doubt a cruel act. I confess that I felt despicable in doing it, but I was desperate.

Hanging there in my miniscule memory bank like notes on that invisible whiteboard is the knowledge that emotions are a powerful tool. They can practically move mountains. Loving someone can drive a person to do almost anything to protect them—everything from fighting a raging bear to battling muggers on a street corner. Love can drive an otherwise timid individual to avenge hurts to a spouse or child. Anger can break decades-old bonds of friendship and even cause wars between countrymen. I needed Anders to act, so I played on his emotions, counting on his anger at me and his love for his son to motivate his decisions.

It had suddenly occurred to me that if I could persuade him to move those tires and find Jasper Fresno's remains, it would prove that he could trust my word about the vampire. It would maybe provide the extra push he needed to ignore the letter of the law. Maybe if I hurt him a little now, it would save lives. Anders would understand that he had to act, and he had to do it while the sun was still up—probable cause or no probable cause. That was my hope, and I clung to it desperately as I sprinted through the main office toward the front entrance carrying his beloved baseball.

Relying on my words alone would get me nowhere. Simply telling him that I knew where Fresno's remains were located after all these years because the man's ghost pointed me in the right direction would only serve to get me more cross-eyed, disbelieving looks. It might get me locked up, but I had to force Anders' hand.

I heard the sheriff roar as I rounded Gator's desk. It wasn't a yell; it was an actual roar born of panic, pain, and anger. I had poked a sleeping beast, and his teeth were ready to take a pound of flesh. He would be on my heels as fast as he could make his large body move. I had no time to waste.

Gator had left his cruiser keys on a tray next to his computer; I grabbed them and tossed them into the fish tank next to the reception counter. I wanted to slow him down but not stop him. I wanted him to follow me, but not catch me too fast. It was a timing thing. They needed to see where I was going but not apprehend me until I reached my destination.

Out of the corner of my eye, I saw Judy Steinkamp standing behind her piles of reports. "What the hell?" she said. "What's going on?"

"Doc, what're you doing?" Gator sputtered. "Where ya going?"

I rounded the counter and was at the front exit before the sheriff managed to open his office door. "Get him," he screamed, rattling the windows. I dared not slow down.

Baseball in hand, I ran past the small post office and was sprinting along Highway 257 toward the main gate of the junkyard within seconds. My target was just ahead. I had to reach it before someone cut me off with the front bumper of a patrol car.

"Doc, stop," Gator called after me.

Sunlight glinted off twisted metal. There was a slight wind hitting my face. Traffic was light, so I angled across the road. When I reached the far side, I glanced back to check on the pursuit that I knew was coming. Judy and Gator were standing on the walk at the front of the post office. The sheriff's cruiser was nosing to the road. I turned on my afterburners and pushed even harder toward the scrapyard's main gate, following the white stripe along the edge of the road. The baseball swung wildly up and down as my right hand pumped the air.

A siren kicked on. A thought came from some unknown place deep in my subconscious, something about being careful what you ask for. It must have been some random memory. If this reckless plan didn't work out, I figured I might not make it to midnight before the event of my untimely death.

Tires squealed as I reached the wide-open gate of the automotive graveyard. A large flatbed truck was leaving, making a right turn onto the highway. It gave me a few more seconds, and I made the most of them, darting straight toward my planned destination—that pile of tires next to the car crusher. If nothing else, I'd reveal Jasper Fresno's body before Anders sent me to join him on the other side.

As I passed the squat little building that apparently housed the office, the two goons that'd escorted me off the lot earlier were lounging in lawn chairs, sipping something suspicious from red plastic cups. The crowbars were leaning against the whitewashed stone wall. I waved the baseball and smiled as I ran by. "Afternoon boys," I sputtered between gasps for air.

"Hey! Where do you think you're going?" said one.

"Come back here," said the other.

They joined the chase as the police cruiser entered the lot, its siren drowning out the sound of the destructive machinery. My heart was slamming, my mind racing. I now had an entourage.

A massive fork truck entered my path. I ducked under the blades and slid to the far side. The guy saw me and stopped short, blocking the two guards and whoever was driving the sheriff's car. I assumed the sheriff was behind the wheel, but I hadn't paused long enough to see for sure. I hoped it was him.

I pushed further ahead as my pursuers waited for the industrial junk mover to get out of the way. They were still fifty feet behind me when I rounded the last pile of destroyed cars. There it was. The Mount Everest of rubber. Jasper's secret tomb.

As I began my climb, the cruiser stopped behind me. Of all the various skills my journal described, scampering up a slick pile of tires with a baseball in one hand wasn't mentioned. Still, I found it within my repertoire. It was like I'd been born to climb used wheel tread. I reached the top and looked down just as Rick Anders slammed his car door, joined by goons with crowbars.

The car-crushing machine next door was smashing someone's old sedan, which made it difficult to hear what Rick was saying, but I got the gist from the scowl on his face. His eyes were like laser pinpoints burning holes through my chest.

Finally, after the sedan was a pancake and the noise subsided, Anders called up to me, "Doc, I don't know what's gotten into you, but if you have any idea what's good for you, you'll come down here and give me that baseball." At that point, I was pretty sure that wouldn't really be good for me. In fact, the chances of something good happening to me any time soon had all fallen to zero. "I'm not playing around," he added, as if I had any doubt.

Anders stood at the foot of the rubber mountain, hands on his utility belt. The human junkyard dogs with the metal rods loomed on either side of him. Gator pulled up and joined the party. It wasn't long before the bald guy that ran the place came along, riding on a dirty golfcart. Ronnie was driving.

"It's Moon-boy! Hey, get your ass on down here, Moon-boy." Ronnie was maintaining his eloquence.

"What's going on here?" the older man asked. "Sheriff, get that kid down off those tires, and get him off my property. This is the second time today I've found him trespassing back here."

"Workin' on it, Bill," Anders replied.

"I'll climb up there and pull him down for you," Ronnie said. "Happy to do it." He was grinning, and I had no doubt he'd enjoy the challenge. I might've too. In another set of circumstances, it might have been fun to play *King of the Rubber Mountain* with ole Ronnie-boy.

"Don't be stupid, son," Bill replied, proving my theory of family relations. "I'll send the boys up after him." The goons looked at one another. They didn't appear too eager to climb the pile. Agility apparently wasn't their strong suit.

"None of you are going anywhere," Anders stated with authority. "Cool your jets."

I watched my former new best friend, the sheriff, take a deep breath. He seemed to be working quite hard at trying to cool his own jets. For the moment, I held my tongue as I stood in the sun on the top of the pile of tires like I had already won the title of King of Tire Mountain.

I had a good view over the various hills of twisted metal. There were more birds in the piles of junk than I would have expected. They were flitting from perch to perch like little winged spectators. I could see the Quarry Pit's sign. Three cars sat in its lot. Judy Steinkamp was still standing on the sidewalk in front of the post office, hands on her hips, perhaps watching for our return.

Gator joined his boss at the bottom of the rubber rings. They spoke, but I couldn't hear what was said. One said something, and the other shook his head. Then the other replied while the first one shook his head. Maybe it was an idea tennis match? An image entered my mind—maybe a lost memory—of a pitcher and catcher sending signals back and forth about the next pitch. A fitting metaphor considering what had caused this crazy situation.

Still holding the baseball in my right hand, I lifted it to take a closer look. Red stitching, the leather still bright white and only scuffed in a couple of places. The lettering of the boy's message was clear and clean, the words formed in even blocks. My mind caught an image of a teenager in a baseball uniform standing near home plate, excited and happy from an important victory. He had a pen in his right hand and the ball in his left. Rick grabbed him and hugged him. The vision was brief but strong. Just then my footing wavered on the tires; I almost fell.

"Doc," Anders called up to me. He paused and took a deep breath, reining himself in, I supposed. "Look, you need to come on back down here. Right now. I'm angry at you. There's no getting around it. Very angry. But you haven't done anything yet that we can't eventually get past. If you don't damage that baseball, we can still work this out. I told you what it means to me."

"Sheriff, I'll come down," I answered, "but first I need you to listen to what I have to say. Then I need you to promise to do something for me."

Anders took another deep breath, working to hold onto whatever patience he'd maintained so far. "What exactly do you want to tell me that you haven't already said? And I'm not in much of a mood to do favors."

While locking eyes with Bill, the older bald guy in the white dress shirt, the apparent owner of the junkyard, I said, "Jasper Fresno is buried under these tires. I've seen it." I pointed at my head again.

Bill's face went as white as his shirt.

"His truck's down there, too. I want you to unbury him. I want you to know that I really do have the ability to see and know things. That way, you'll know without a doubt that what I'm saying about the monster on the bluff is true. You need to act on my information before it gets dark."

"He's talkin' crazy, Sheriff," Bill stated. "The boy's got to be drugged out of his mind. Don't just stand there and let him yammer. Let me send my crew up to get him."

Anders ignored Bill and addressed me, "I'm not moving any tires today, son. Please just crawl down here. We'll go back to the station and discuss your visions there."

"Nope. Nope. Nope," I said, shaking my head. "We're doing this now. I'm serious, Sheriff. Start pulling tires off this mound, or I'll drop the ball. I don't want to, but I will unless I have your word, and tires start to move." I held the baseball out, dangling it over an opening in a whitewall that said Goodyear on the side.

Anders' stricken face drooped like he'd had a stroke. He clearly was considering his options. He didn't have many. Anything short of compliance, and he'd risk me dropping his prize possession. I had him in a pickle.

"Fine. We'll move some tires if that'll satisfy you enough to come off that pile of rubber."

The sheriff turned to Gator and pointed. "Start pulling tires off. Shove 'em over there," he said, indicating a mountain of twisted metal behind the goons. "You boys help him," he instructed the guys with the crowbars.

Bill's henchmen tossed their metal rods aside and followed Gator to the edge of the rubber slope. They were glaring at me as they moved.

"Stop! You can't do that," Bill shouted. His panicked face told the story. It was like there was a neon sign just under the skin of his forehead flashing *"Guilty, Guilty, Guilty."* He confronted Anders. "This is private property. You've no right to start moving my stuff around."

"Bill, we're not hurting anything, and I'm trying to diffuse the situation. Your machines can put them right back when we're done," Anders said as he grabbed a tire himself, tossing it across the lot toward the new pile they were creating.

"You don't have a warrant," Bill pointed out.

"Why would I need a warrant? I'm not searching for anything. I'm just trying to get that boy off that pile of rubber. Is Jasper Fresno actually under there? Is that why you're so worked up?" The sheriff cocked his head and looked sideways at the junkyard's owner.

Bill was between a rock and a solid slab of granite. If he refused to let them continue, it would lead to a warrant for sure. If he let them go on, they would find Fresno. "Fine," he eventually said. "Do whatever you want." Then, he went silent, staring at Anders as tires began to fly. He looked like a whitewashed statue, frozen in place. Ronnie was silent, too, staring at his dad. Bill's two henchmen were moving tires despite their boss's reaction, tossing them over their shoulders and letting them roll into a new mound.

I had a bird's eye view from my perch as Anders, Gator, and the buffoons dug into the pile. Bill and Ronnie jumped on the golf cart and sped back to the office. I could see the small building over the mounds of junk. Ronnie's Camaro was parked behind the place. They skidded to a stop next to it, jumped out of the cart, climbed into the car, and left in a hurry. The sound of squealing tires reached all the way to where we stood as they pulled onto Highway 257.

Jasper's ghost was standing next to me, perched on a Michelin. I turned and smiled at him, pleased with myself, sure they'd find his truck and then likely his desiccated body. He smiled back—then he stuck his right hand inside my head.

Nine

Journal Excerpts

My plan was a dangerous one, but it may have worked. The sheriff is very angry. He may never forgive me. If I were him, I probably wouldn't.

My guess is confirmed. Ronnie is the junkyard owner's son. He must be. He still hates me, too. I don't like him much either, but Rose said he wasn't always such a nasty person. I can't hate him back. Maybe I'm not so good at hating.

Maybe you can't hate if you can't remember things.

———— • ● • ————

As far as I know, I'd never before had a ghost stick its hand in my head. It would be okay with me if it never happened again. It felt like a cold knife slicing directly into my brain, then attaching itself with tiny, slithering micro threads. Jasper gave me no warning—no "Hey, do you mind if I—." Instead, old shimmering Jasper just assumed I'd be okay with it.

First, I went stiff—head to toe. I no longer had any muscle control, but I could still see, at least at first. The baseball dropped from my fingers. It slipped right out of my hand and fell directly into the hole at the center of the worn-out whitewall I'd been dangling it over. My heart sank with the ball. It wasn't my intention to truly drop or damage the precious item. I meant it only as a threat to force the sheriff to act. It was an idle threat, a bluff.

Speaking of the sheriff, I couldn't look at him, and I mean that literally; my eyes wouldn't move in that direction. Instead, I watched the ball bounce around until it descended out of sight and clanged against something metal, likely the top of Jasper's truck. At least I never heard a splash. I was grateful for that mercy.

My voice worked, but it wasn't me talking. I had no control of my vocal cords. "I. Am. Buried. Here." Those words exited my lips just before my vision blurred and my mind went elsewhere.

* * *

When my eyes refocused, I found myself behind the wheel of a pickup truck, driving along a road lined with trees on both sides. The radio was playing a song— Willie Nelson singing about being on the road again and making music with some friends. It's funny and a little weird, but I recognized the voice.

I had no control over the experience. My vision existed only as a passenger inside who I assumed to be Jasper Fresno. I was seeing what he saw, hearing what he heard, and feeling what he felt.

It was late; the sky was dusky. His headlights were on, but it was that time of the evening when there's still a touch too much daylight for the beams to be effective, but not enough daylight to really see well.

The windows of the truck were down. Wind was blowing through, rustling the hair on Jasper's head. I felt it blowing around. Jasper's elbow was resting on the door, partially extended outside the window. Insects smashed themselves on the windshield. "Damn bugs," he said.

The engine was missing out, popping, and the truck was moving down the road in fits and starts. Coughing. Sputtering. Chugging. "Come on, Bessie," Jasper said. "Just get us home, okay?" Despite the request, the old Ford finally gave up the ghost on a steep hill as it approached a curve. Jasper managed to move it to the berm just before its momentum gave out.

The low light, the forest, and the curve up the hill made seeing anything pretty much impossible. The dim, flickering headlights landed on the pavement ten feet in front of the truck but didn't penetrate much beyond that. Without the engine noise, the crickets, frogs, and insects of the forest sounded like an orchestra tuning up before a concert.

"Well hellfire burn it all," Jasper cursed. His right hand shifted the transmission into park. His head turned; my vision followed. On the passenger seat was a plastic shopping bag, probably the part for the truck he'd just bought at the auto-supply store in French Lick. A closed, half-empty bottle of Fresca rested on its side next to the bag. He grabbed the soda, twisted the lid, and lifted it for a sip. I really wanted to taste that drink, but my vision only allowed for a hint of the flavor. Apparently, unlike the senses of hearing and sight, the tastebuds don't transfer information as effectively through visions across the decades. This one didn't, anyway.

Jasper's hands resealed the now-empty bottle and tossed it behind the seat. "Screw it. Guess I'll walk," Jasper mumbled. The eyes moved to a plastic catchall tray sitting on the hump in the floorboard. It held a beanbag ashtray half filled with butts, a dead French fry, about a hundred layers of grime, plus a fat, trifold wallet. He grabbed the wallet, then leaned back so he could stuff it in his front right pants pocket.

I was expecting him to grab a cell phone. Then I remembered that what I was seeing happened in the days when cell phones were a new thing. Not everyone had one, and Jasper was a loner. He had no one to call anyway.

Jasper checked the rearview mirrors. The road was curving away behind him. Another blind curve. Not a great spot for a breakdown, but the road was quiet. No one had passed the pickup in either direction since my vision joined the ride. He reached in his shirt pocket and removed his pack of smokes, pulled one, and lit it with the lighter built into the truck's dash.

I've never been a smoker—I think— so in that moment, I was glad my visions were mostly visual and auditory. Even with the reduced sense of taste and smell, I found the experience unpleasant.

With the cigarette hanging from his lips, he checked the glove box. I think he was looking for a flashlight, but I can't be sure. After a moment, he gave up and popped it shut.

After turning on his blinkers, Jasper opened the driver's side door and stepped out into the fading light of the evening. He had to slam the pickup's door twice to get it to close. Jasper didn't bother locking it, probably because he didn't think there was anything in it worth stealing. Then he started walking up the hill along the left edge of the road toward the curve ahead of him.

He hadn't gone fifty feet when a vehicle rounded that upcoming curve going downhill way too fast. No headlights and no warning. Jasper saw it coming but just a moment too late. His eyes registered a tow truck. For a half second, he felt a flash of relief, but then realized it wasn't coming to his rescue.

The truck left the pavement and Jasper dodged to his right, but the driver overcorrected, swerved, and veered back across the road. Jasper Fresno's torso smashed into the center of the truck's grill, flipped up, glanced off the windshield, and flew into the tow mechanism hanging off the rear. He landed headfirst in the center of the road.

I felt every bit of it, grateful for the muted sense of touch and pain in my visions. Even so, I can't adequately describe the trauma and the terror.

Red taillights illuminated the road as the driver slammed his brakes. Footsteps. Jasper was on his back, staring upward toward the treetops. The sky was just lighter than the trees themselves with a hint of pink hanging on from the sunset. The moon was already up. A man leaned into my vision.

When I saw the man through Jasper's eyes, at first, I thought it was Ronnie. Same hair, same build, same eyes. Then I realized that this happened before Ronnie was born. This was Bill. This was Ronnie's dad.

"Are you okay," Bill asked. It was a stupid question, as Jasper lay there all broken up. "Oh, my God! Holy hell. What were you doing in the road?"

"Help me," Jasper croaked, barely audible. As he breathed, blood gurgled in his throat. He choked and coughed it up. It drained across his face, warm on his cheeks.

Bill's frantic eyes glanced up the road. He looked down the road. He pranced toward his truck, stopped, and then stumbled back. He was clearly in a panic.

Jasper followed him with his eyes. They were the only things he could move except for his fingers; they were opening and closing, clawing at the air. "Help me, please," Jasper repeated, spitting blood with each syllable.

"How? I don't know what to do. I'm sorry. I'm so sorry."

"Get…help." More blood flooded his mouth. I could taste the muted flavor of iron across the years.

Jasper stared into Bill's bloodshot eyes and desperate face. As he did, his vision began to retreat. Bill drifted farther away, getting smaller and smaller, shrinking even as he stood there. Jasper's pain receded too, lessening, a welcome relief. The darkness within his vision widened and deepened until finally it enveloped him. The road, the forest, and the tow truck driver were gone. Then the darkness exploded into a bright light that flashed across his vision. It was too bright, too brilliant. Jasper Fresno died.

— • ● • —

When I returned to myself, I was on the ground leaning against Gator's cruiser. A lot of me hurt, but it was nothing compared to the pain Jasper had felt. Gator was leaning over me, holding a cold pack against the side of my aching head. There were scrapes on my hands and elbows.

"You okay, Doc?" He leaned over further so he could see into my eyes, probably checking my pupils. Perhaps concerned about a concussion.

"I'm not sure." I said, lifting my hands to inspect the torn skin of my palms. "I think so. Nothing feels broken." The memory of feeling broken on the roadway pavement was fresh in my mind.

"You took a good tumble down that pile of tires and fell right off the edge we'd made in the side. Lucky you didn't break your neck. Did you lose your balance or something?"

"No. I was off watching Jasper Fresno's death

from thirty years ago." I leaned so I could see past Gator. The goons had uncovered the side of Jasper's truck. The sheriff was on top, throwing tires aside, likely looking for the baseball that I'd dropped. Sharing some of the details of my vision with Gator, I said, "Ronnie's dad killed him. Hit him with a tow truck. It was an accident, a terrible, horrible accident. I saw it all. Sort of lived through it, you might say. He must've panicked and hid Jasper's body and truck under the tires to cover it up."

"There's a body in there," one of the goons yelled, cupping his hands on the dirty glass. "Looks all dried up."

Gator left me sitting there on my butt in the dirt and joined the muscle-bound guy. He pulled his flashlight from his belt and shined it through the grimy passenger-side glass. "There's old Jasper, alright."

Anders, standing on the hood of the pickup, held up the baseball he'd pulled from inside a Goodrich radial at about the same moment Gator illuminated the corpse. "I've got it," he exclaimed as he tossed the rubber ring aside. At that moment, he apparently also saw Jasper's mummified face staring at him through the windshield because he jerked back and dropped the baseball. It rolled off the hood, landing in the dirt next to an old Yokohama. "Geez," he exclaimed.

After crouching to peer into the cab of the old truck, Anders hopped off the hood and retrieved the baseball. He picked it out of the dirt, held it up, brushed it off, and examined all sides. Satisfied, he stuffed it in one of his oversized, cargo pockets.

He was smiling from ear to ear as he approached me, obviously relieved. His smile disappeared, though, when he stopped and peered down at my miserable self. "Well, it seems you've solved a thirty-year-old mystery—" he said, pausing briefly. "By committing yet another crime of your own. What am I going to do with you, Doc?"

"I'm sorry," I said. "Didn't mean to drop it. I just wanted you to look under the tires, so you could find Jasper."

Sheriff Anders stared at me for what felt like an hour but was only a few seconds. I didn't know if he could see how guilty I felt, but I tried on my best sad-puppy face. "I wanted to prove to you that my visions are real. I needed you to believe me, so you'd act on the vampire up on the bluff."

"Well, I guess you've convinced me, sure enough," he said.

"When I accidentally dropped the ball and fell, I was having another vision. I saw Jasper's death. As I just told Gator, that guy you called Bill—he killed Jasper. It was an accident, though. He didn't murder him. I saw the whole thing."

"I knew you had to be seeing something. You went all rigid, and your eyes rolled up in their sockets. If it was an accident, why'd he hide him? Did you see that?"

"I don't know for sure. The guy looked like Ronnie does now. He was panicking. Desperate. Maybe he'd been drinking, I dunno, but it was definitely an accident. Jasper's truck broke down on some dark road. He'd started walking. Bill… That's his name, right?" Anders nodded. "Well, he came around a corner and hit him in the dark. The impact flipped Jasper up and over Bill's truck. He landed on the pavement all broken up. Jasper died there in the road with Bill looking down at him."

"Can you stand up?" Anders asked. He stuck his hand out to help me. I took his offer, and he pulled me to my feet. Then, he spun me around, pulled my arm behind me, and placed a metal bracelet on my wrist. He yanked my other hand around and connected the handcuffs.

"You're arresting me?"

"I'm detaining you while I think about it…about the list of potential charges. Trespassing…twice. Maybe three times. Vagrancy, if that law's still on the books. Theft. Criminal Mischief. Maybe Fleeing, too." His hard expression then hardened some more. "You know, I don't need to think about it. I'm going ahead with an arrest. Maybe some time in jail will give you better judgment." He motioned Gator over. "Deputy, read this young man his rights and take him back to the station. Lock him in a cell, and this time I do mean for you to lock it." He turned his back to me and marched toward Jasper's truck.

Gator peered at me and shrugged. "You have the right to remain silent," he said as he pointed at his cruiser's rear door. "Anything you say can and will be used against you." He continued until he'd finished my Miranda warning. "Sorry, Doc," he added at the end.

"Sheriff?" I called out before dropping into Gator's rear seat. Anders paused and turned back. "Do you believe me now? About the vampire and the garage?"

"I do."

"Will you go in? Before dark?"

"We'll discuss it when I get back to the station."

That answer didn't give me the warm and fuzzies.

• ● •

Gator and I didn't speak during the short drive to the jail. He brought me in the rear door and marched me into the office where Judy Steinkamp gave me the stink-eye. I didn't need to stay under her condemning gaze long because the deputy directed me down the corridor to the cellblock. He stuck me back in the one I'd slept in the previous night, but this time he closed it, locking me inside. I gripped the bars and peered at him, trying to give off a forlorn vibe.

"Sorry Doc," he said again, pulling off his hat and scratching his head, "but you did sorta do this to yourself."

"Yeah," I answered. "I guess I did." I backed away from the bars and sat on my bunk, slumped over with my elbows on my knees. A helpless feeling swept over me. My goal was to get that vampire dealt with before the sun went down and all hell broke loose. Instead, all I'd managed to do was convince the sheriff that it was a real threat, something he already knew based on the missing people. I got myself locked up, too. Yep, I was quite an accomplished jailbird.

"I don't know for sure, but I think he'll let you go," Gator said, breaking into my tormented thoughts. "After all, no real harm was done, and you did solve a very old mystery."

There was that. I managed to find a way to reveal where Jasper's body had been stashed for thirty years. That was something. Yet, if the sheriff let the sun go down on that creature in the shipping container, fresh blood would be splattered all over this little town. "I just want you guys to kill that monster holed up in that garage and do it before the sun sets. That's all I care about. After that, we can deal with my charges. Throw the book at me for all I care. If you kill that vampire, I don't care what you do to me."

"I hear you," Gator said. He paused for a moment. "I need to go. Is there anything I can get you?"

"Can I have my journal and a pen?"

He left, then returned moments later, handing my request through the bars. "Don't make me regret trusting you with this ink pen." Then, he retreated to the office, and I sat on the cot with my feet dangling. I needed to record the last couple of hours, but my mind kept going back to the locked garage on the bluff. Had I done enough to convince the sheriff to act? It had to be enough. I didn't have anything more.

I flipped open the notebook, clicked the pen, preparing to write, before letting my mind flow out, exploring, probing, thinking about the killer in the mansion's garage. Closing my eyes, I felt a part of me drift upward. Behind my eyelids, I could see as I passed through the roof of the station and floated over the trees. Drifting, I leaned forward and began to move over the top of the surrounding forest. I looked up and caught sight of the ominous mansion on the ridge. Suddenly, my vision went dark, and I found myself again inside that locked container on the cliff above Cutters Notch.

I didn't know I had the ability to instigate an out-of-body experience. I'm not even sure how I made it happen. Yet, my body was sitting in the jail and my mind was elsewhere, having located the creature I was thinking about. I made a mental note to jot that down in my journal, so I'd see it and remember that I could do it in the future.

I was standing inside one end of the shipping container. Candlelight flickered across the corrugated-metal walls coming from a series of fat, white columns of wax positioned around the container. I could hear the candles popping and cracking in the cavernous space. They were scented. Lavender.

I don't know if I'll ever get used to being in one place and then suddenly finding myself in another. If the vision of my death comes true, I won't need to. It's disconcerting—kind of like a mental sense of vertigo. If I were actually standing, I might have gotten dizzy, maybe even stumbled and fell.

A scan of my journal earlier revealed two types of visions I tended to experience. One was a peek into the future, usually involving my untimely death. The other was a view to the past, usually someone else's untimely death. This vision I was experiencing inside the shipping container was something new. I had sought the vampire out, and it had invited me in, welcoming me to a little chat. Not the future. Not the past. More like the *there-and-now* with the ability to communicate.

Roughly ten feet away, between two especially large candles, sat a darkly robed figure. I could see the top, front side of the chair's seatback—dark, ornately-carved wood—extending above the vampire's hooded head. He wasn't looking at me. Rather, he was peering downward, as if deep in thought. His elbows were perched on the arms of the chair, and the tips of his long, bony fingers were joined into a spire before him, as if he were praying.

This time, I could see his feet. No shoes. Like his hands, his feet were bony with long toes. The nails were extended and shaped into claw-like points.

Finally, the creature turned his eyes upward, the yellow orbs illuminating his face, enhanced by the twin candles nearby. The skin of his face was gray with wrinkles, and it drooped a bit. He looked hungry. His closed mouth formed a scowl, giving him an angry countenance. When he finally spoke, the words passed through jagged teeth like wind through steel bars.

"D.R. Moon, welcome to my home. They refer to you as Doc, I believe."

Well, that's not a good sign. The vampire knows my name. The thought of fleeing Cutters Notch occurred to me again, but I knew I couldn't, being locked up in the jail like a bird in a snare.

His accent was definitely French as he cut to the chase. "You wish my demise? You want your local sheriff to storm my home before the sun sets? You think that if I am attacked in the light of the day, I can be killed?"

To this point, I hadn't spoken. Frankly, I was scared my voice wouldn't function. I knew intellectually that I wasn't physically in the room, but on a metaphysical and emotional level, I was in the presence of a deadly force to be reckoned with. One that very well could be the end of me within the next few hours. "That was kind of my thinking, yeah."

"Why? Do I not have a right to live, to survive? To enjoy the spoils of my existence? To flourish, even? Do not all creatures hunt, kill, and eat to survive? Am I so different? Like you humans, I have needs. Over time, I have acquired financial resources, but unlike you, I cannot purchase my food in a grocery store. When I grow hungry and my supplies are low, I must hunt, and humans are the only prey that truly nourishes me. I feed on your kind merely to survive."

I suppose he had a philosophical point but humans, being traditionally at the top of the food chain, don't particularly like to forfeit that position. We are the hunters, not the hunted. We might plunder one another, but we don't want some other being plundering us.

In a battle between my intellect and my emotions, I tried to focus on logic rather than fear. He couldn't hurt me, at least not in that moment. "You do have a point," I conceded, "but we also have a right to protect ourselves from you, the hunter."

He laughed. It was loud and high-pitched, sort of a shriek. Then he rose to his feet. The top of his hood brushed the ceiling of the metal box in which we stood. I would say he stepped toward me, but it was really more of a drift, smooth and swift. Logic and fear battled within me, and the fear was winning out.

"Soon, Doc, the sun will drop below the horizon, and I will be free to roam the countryside. I'm hungry, and I will feed tonight. Have no doubt. In fact, I will feast like a king at his own coronation. When I am sated, those who survive will sop up the leftover blood, and I will have moved on." He grinned, displaying the mating rows of pointed teeth. His yellow eyes, like twin suns, bored into my soul.

He pointed a bony finger at me. "I will come for you tonight," he continued. "I can sense you even now as you sit in that tiny cell in the sheriff's station, locked in much as I'm locked in here. Tonight, when my hunger is satisfied, I will turn my attention to you. You will truly see me then, not just images in your mind. In that moment, you will know the true fear of being one of the hunted." When he'd finished his soliloquy, he lifted both hands, palms out, and shoved the air toward me.

My consciousness flung backward through the wall of the shipping container, across the edge of the bluff, over the tops of the trees, and down to my cell on the edge of town. I opened my eyes again, still in my locked cubicle with a pen in my hand, drenched in sweat. To top it all, I'd wet my pants. Not exactly one of my prouder moments, but it happened. At least my journal wasn't lying on my lap.

Ten

Journal Excerpts

Jasper stuck his hand inside my head. It was so freaking cold,

like squirming icicles. I'd be okay if it never happened to me again.

I'm back in the jail. This time, I'm under arrest.

I was probing for the vampire, searching with my mind, when he pulled me into his lair. He's intelligent and speaks with an accent.

The vampire thinks he's entitled to kill people, and he's coming for me.

I ought to run as fast as I can right out the other side of Cutters Notch.

— • ● • —

My journal doesn't record any previous examples of my wetting my pants. Maybe that side effect of vision-influenced terror is new to me. Or maybe I was simply too embarrassed by any previous experiences to write them down. I hesitate to record it now, but the truth needs to be told. Besides, as it turns out, that humiliating experience turned out to be somewhat fortuitous.

As embarrassing as it was at that moment, I needed help. Being secured in a jail cell afforded me limited options. I had no spare pants within reach, and no one wants to sit in their urine, just waiting to dry out. There's nothing like peeing one's pants to eliminate whatever ego a guy might have left. At least it hadn't happened in front of Rose.

"Gator? Sheriff? Someone?" I stood up, feeling the warm liquid work its way down my legs, and leaned into the cell door as I called down the hallway. "I need some help. Can someone help me? Please."

I didn't know which would be worse, to have the sheriff or the office administrator, Judy Steinkamp, come to my rescue. Hopefully it would be Gator as he was likely the only friend I had left in the Sheriff's Department of Cutters Notch. "Please help me." I sounded pathetic even to myself.

It took a few tries, but it was Judy who finally answered my call. "What do you want, kid?" Based on her tone of voice, I'd lost any previous sympathy she may have felt for me.

"I've sorta made a mess of myself."

"Wha'd you do?" She huffed into the hallway outside my cell. Being gruff and abrupt were likely traits intrinsic to working in a jail and dealing with troublemakers. I might be unique, but I was still a troublemaker.

"I had a nightmare, I guess." It really wasn't a guess. "And I woke up all wet." This came out rather sheepishly. It was more than a nightmare. However, considering my current state of personal need, it wouldn't help my plea to go spouting off to Judy about having visionary conversations with a monster on the bluff.

"Goodness, boy. Is this something that happens to you a lot?" Judy was probably envisioning a need to keep supplying me with fresh pants and bedclothes. She stood and looked at my sorry self for a few moments, hands on her hips.

I didn't try to write shame all over my face; it plastered itself there all on its own.

"All right," she finally said, apparently resigned to the situation. "I'll bring you a fresh set of clothes and change the bed out, too."

"Thank you," I replied, and moved to the corner to wait.

A few moments later, she unlocked the cell door and tossed me the orange clothes. "Go to the men's room and change." She handed me a plastic bag. "Put your wet pants in this."

"You're not worried about me running off?"

She stopped in her tracks, cocked her head to one side, and glared at me. "No. Go change and come right back. Don't screw around. If you try something cute like running off, I'll rip your fingernails off one at a time, and I'll be smiling all the while."

Maybe this was just her way of intimidating me, but between her grin and the look in her eyes, I believed her threat. In that moment, I was almost as afraid of Judy Steinkamp as I was the yellow-eyed killer in the cape. I'd done my bad deed for the day, so I followed her instructions to the letter as quickly as possible. I caught sight of a clock on my way to the john, and let's just say that I could feel the sunset speeding toward me.

"Where is everyone?" I asked as I returned in dry clothes—my normal shirt and a new set of orange jail trousers. The new pants were roomy but felt a little rough on the inside. I carried the plastic bag containing my wet stuff out in front of me as if it were dangerous.

She took the bag of pee pants and answered my question as she walked. "Follow me," she said as she headed toward the laundry area. "Everyone's out looking for Bill Castle."

"Bill Castle?" I had a good idea who that was, but I'd never actually heard his last name.

"The guy you implicated with your little stunt with the baseball." She stopped and glared at me again. "That was really stupid, you know. If you ever pull something like that with me, I'll disembowel you with a clothes hanger." She was smiling again when she said it. I wondered if she might be speaking from experience.

Judy had a scary way of communicating. Her words made me want to fall in line and do whatever she wanted—no questions and no smart-ass responses. It seemed the safest option. I averted my eyes from the daggers she was throwing.

"Even if it was an accident like you told the sheriff," she continued. "Bill hid a body on his property for thirty years. The circumstances must be investigated, and he has to answer for his actions one way or another, accident or not." In the laundry room, Judy tipped the bag up and dropped my pants into the washer, continuing to speak as she did the chore. "Did you take everything out of these pants? No random crap in the pockets?"

"Yeah," I confirmed. "I checked 'em over good before I slunk back out here to give them to you."

After loading the machine, she continued with the update. "Well, apparently when it became clear that old Fresno was going to be uncovered, Bill had his boy run him home. From there, both of 'em disappeared. Skipped town, I suppose. Rick's got the whole team searching for him."

My heart sank as my anxiety rose. I'd wanted to prove the accuracy of my visions to the sheriff, so he'd take his team up that bluff and kill that creature under the light of day. Instead, I'd caused him to launch a manhunt for a completely different situation, pulling all his resources away from protecting the town from the vampire.

"He had me put a BOLO out for their vehicles," she added as we headed back to the office. "I doubt they'll get far. The State Police will probably catch 'em." Her tone softened as she spoke, lessening my inherent fear of her serial-killer potential.

Weird. Despite her scary rhetoric, as I was following her around the office like a puppy, I was developing a bond with her. She was the grumpy grandma that talked mean but loved you anyway. I was growing attached.

The bell at the front door dinged as Judy took her seat. I turned to observe Rose making her entrance and striding right around the reception counter as if she owned the place. She wore a white, sleeveless blouse with a brown pattern that matched her freckles very well. I couldn't help noticing that her legs were freckled too—right up until they disappeared into her shorts. Maybe she was twice my age; maybe she wasn't, but she was quite a vision to behold.

"Judy, I heard you had my friend, Doc, under arrest. What gives?"

"He did it to himself, Rose. Pushed the sheriff too far. I doubt he'll be charged, but Rick locked him up, mostly for his own safety. Seems he can't help but get himself in trouble."

Rose forced me into a hug, something that didn't take much effort. Then she positioned herself directly in front of Judy's desk. "How about you release him to me? I'll take charge of him, keep him outta trouble."

"I can't do that," Judy replied. "Sheriff says he stays here. The only reason he isn't in a cell is—."

I cut her off, trying to avoid revealing my "accident" to the attractive, apparently middle-aged woman with the waves of mesmerizing reddish-brown curls draping her freckled shoulders. "I wanted to talk, so she let me out for a bit."

Judy glared at me again. "You in the habit of rudely interrupting people?"

"Sorry," I said, remembering the coat hanger threat.

Judy must have understood my embarrassment, though, because she didn't complete her explanation to Rose. After she finished scaring me with her eyes, she brought the discussion to a close. "Rose, I can't release him. Is there something else you need? I have work to do." Judy's hands began shifting papers around on her busy-looking desk.

"Can I visit with him?"

Judy studied Rose for a few moments, considering the request. "Sure. Seems safe enough. Go sit in the conference room."

• ● •

Once again, I found myself alone in a room with the beautiful, mysterious girl of my dreams, but this time without her spectral roommates. There was a coffee station on a credenza along the inside wall of the conference room. The urn was half full. It smelled good. "Want a cup?" I asked Rose.

"Naw, it'll keep me awake."

If I lived in a house with thirty or so ghosts, some of whom liked to ram their fingers into brains, I wouldn't sleep much either, coffee or no coffee. Fresno's fingers had felt like icepicks as they took over my brainwaves. Once was enough.

Ceramic cups sat upside down on a towel nearby. I picked one, put three packs of granulated sugar in the bottom, topped it off with some powdered creamer, and then filled the cup with some brew. After taking a sip, I took a seat directly across the table from the woman who'd captured my imagination.

Could she really be forty years old? It occurred to me that if she were able to disguise her age so effectively, maybe I could too. After all, I didn't really know how old I was. Maybe I was older than I looked. I guess the mind concocts whatever rationalization it needs to get what it wants.

I chose to ignore the memory of watching ghosts stick their hands into the side of her head. Finding that ignoring and forgetting were two different things, I couldn't quite wipe the experience from my mind. Based on my journal, I'd forget it by the next day, but at that moment, the vivid experience remained, despite my efforts to block it from my mind.

"I suppose you being locked up is a result of how you solved your predicament?" She smiled. Her red lipstick accented the slight hint of red in her hair, leaving her lips looking soft and moist.

"A direct result," I answered. "I guess it worked because they found old Jasper Fresno right where I knew he was buried." My eyes drifted from her lips to her neckline before I forced them unwillingly back to her eyes. "I thought you were working this afternoon. You get off early?"

"No, I got off at four. I ran home to change, then came right over here."

She mentioned the time, and my anxiety slammed back to the forefront of my brain. Tick, tick, tick. Time was speeding unhindered directly toward my demise, not to mention the threat to the whole town. As if to add emphasis, a glare hit my eyes, the sun coming through the western windows of the room as it slowly sank toward the horizon.

"When the sheriff returns, I'm going to get you out

of this place."

"Just like that? You think the sheriff will simply let me go because you said so?"

"Yes," she replied, confidence evident in her bright green eyes. "He'll do it if I ask him. Then we can have dinner, and you can forget all about this trouble."

"I don't think forgetting is in the cards this evening." I didn't add that I'd totally forget everything if I somehow made it to tomorrow. In a flash, my earliest memory came to mind from yesterday evening at about this time. I was walking down the side of a road. Everything before that moment was hazy, kind of like residual chalk on an erased board. As I took each step in those memories, the one before it disappeared into a haze of nothingness.

Rose's hands were on the table, red nails to match her lips. On impulse, I reached over and took them into my own. "I need to tell you something, Rose."

She smiled again. "Okay?"

"You're in danger. This whole town is in danger."

The smile disappeared from her face, and her eyes grew intense. The muscles in her hands tensed up as she gripped my fingers. "What do you mean? In danger, how?"

"You know that man who disappeared a few weeks ago?"

"Yes."

"And the three teens who've disappeared since then?"

"Uh huh."

"You're gonna think I'm crazy—" I peered down at the table in front of me. Suddenly, I couldn't bring myself to meet her eyes. I didn't want to see the disbelief when it showed up in them. "There's a creature…a monster. It stays in a shipping container during the day, inside a locked garage at an abandoned home up on the bluff." By this time, I figured she was glaring at me, shocked that I'd concoct such a crazy story. Maybe about to drop my hands and walk straight out the door.

Rather than rejecting me and making a hasty exit, she began to rub my hands with her thumbs. "Go on, honey."

I took a chance to glance at her eyes. Intense, serious, and completely engaged. "Best I can tell, it comes out about once a week to feed. It was out last night, but it missed its target, so it's hungry. On top of that, it knows I'm onto it, that its cover is blown. It even knows my name."

"How can it know that?"

"It has somehow been watching me. I have these…these…well, I guess you'd call them visions. I see things. That's how I knew Fresno was under the tires, and how I saw the ghosts in your house. I can see the monster in my visions. I guess it has a similar power. The beast sought me out even as I was probing for it. Pulled my mind right into its den and confronted me." I paused. My arms were shaking. "He said he was coming for me…tonight."

Rose stood, came around the table, and pulled me into another hug. As scared as I was, I liked it. No reason to lie. "You can come stay at my place," she said. "The spirits will block it out. It won't find you there."

It wasn't a bad idea. An alternative to fleeing town. But just because Ronnie Castle couldn't see me standing right in front of him on Rose's driveway didn't mean that monster couldn't peer past the ghostly camouflage. Still, it was worth keeping her suggestion in mind.

I pulled away, needing a clear mind, and having her skin touching mine didn't allow for that. My obsession with this possibly older woman wasn't useful in my current predicament. Instead, I refilled my coffee cup. I knew I wasn't going to be sleeping any time soon and the caffeine boost would help me focus. "Thanks for the invitation, but I can't take you up on that suggestion, Rose," I eventually said.

"Why not?" She was pouting. It was the cutest thing. "You'd be safe, and we'd have a nice evening," she added with an alluring grin. Tempting. Very tempting.

"If he doesn't find me, he'll take it out on the rest of the town. I'm going to have to face him, I guess—a showdown of sorts. It'll either be me or him still standing when the sun rises tomorrow." I walked to the window and gazed out. "I really need the sheriff to go take him out while the sun's still in the sky. He's weaker then. Vulnerable. Then, maybe we can avoid the whole mess."

"Ain't gonna happen, Doc," Rick said as his frame filled the doorway. He motioned for me to follow him. He wasn't smiling, but at least he didn't seem angry anymore. "Come on, kid. Let's talk."

— • ● • —

Once again, I found myself sitting in the sheriff's office with him at his desk, elbows on the top, hands crossed. The baseball was missing though, probably safely locked in his desk somewhere. The only other difference was my orange pants.

"Why're you wearing jail clothes?" asked Anders.

"That thing invaded my mind, and I pissed myself." I was no longer desperate or embarrassed; I was angry.

He nodded at me. "Doc, now that I've had a couple of hours to settle down, I'm no longer considering ripping your arms off at the sockets and then beating you to death with them."

"That's a relief," I said. "Now, all I have to worry about is a giant monster with yellow eyes and sharp, vicious-looking teeth ripping my throat out at midnight. Tonight. Just a few hours from now."

The sheriff continued as if I'd said nothing at all. He leaned back, rocking in his desk chair. "After all, you did solve a thirty-year-old mystery. No one would've ever thought to look for Jasper Fresno under all those old tires. He's been there for so long; he may have been there for thirty more years before anyone found him." Anders paused, staring at me. "That said, if you ever touch that baseball again, all bets are off. You got that?"

He really *had* considered ripping my arms off at the shoulders. "Yessir," I replied.

Anders stood, hands on his utility belt, and stared out the window, the same one I'd been staring through earlier before I swiped the ball. He was twice my size, muscular, built like a human tank. A red line showed through his short hair where the strap of his hat had rested on his scalp.

"Look, kid, I'm not oblivious to the situation at hand. I know what you're worried about. I'm worried about it, too." He turned to face me. "Having said that, I'm bound by rules, protocol, laws. I can't just break into someone's locked property. It may look completely abandoned, but it's actually owned by people—a corporation in New York. If you're wrong, my head would be on the block."

"I'm not wrong. Look, you dug into those tires," I pointed out, trying my hand at logic. "Where were your rules and protocol then?"

"I probably did stretch things, but I could make the excuse that I was in pursuit of a fleeing person…you. And I wanted to retrieve the baseball you stole, which I saw fall into the stack of tires. It gave me probable cause. Plus, Bill gave me permission right before he fled."

"Did you find Castle? Arrest him?" I hadn't been back in the office area since Rose had shown up. Was he back there in one of the cells?

"He's disappeared. Probably decided to blow town when he realized I was going to find Fresno's buried body. All my deputies are searching. We put a BOLO out to the surrounding counties and the Indiana State Police. We'll find him."

"Ronnie?"

"He's missing too. We're not looking to arrest him, though. This all happened before he was born, but we've checked his house and his girl's mom's place. The team is checking any place his dad might hide. He probably joined Bill on the run, or they're holed up somewhere."

I stood also. Anders had the window to the outside, so I gazed through the window in the door. Rose was still out there, sitting quietly on a wooden chair next to the fish tank on the far wall. She smiled and gave me a little wave. Her bright green eyes sparkled. This attraction could lead somewhere if I wasn't careful. What little I knew of myself didn't indicate a tendency to err on the side of caution. "Sheriff, you do believe me, don't you? About the vampire?"

"I do."

"So, you must have a plan. Some sort of idea of what you're going to do to protect the people around here." My mind flashed an image—Rose, her body leaning against the glass doors of the General Store, her throat ripped out. The vision changed and I saw a river of blood flowing down the gutter in front of the library. The librarian lying on the steps in her white blouse, now crimson with her own spilt blood, her reading glasses swimming in a pool on her chest. The images were brief, but intense—no doubt placed in my mind by the creature itself. "You have to have a plan," I stated as strongly as I could without shouting.

Anders returned to his desk and lowered his large frame into the faux-leather chair. It squeaked as he sat. As he watched me standing there by his office door, he casually opened a drawer and retrieved his prize baseball. He read the inscription written in his son's handwriting before placing it back inside and reclosing the drawer. Then, he took a sip of Coke from a sweating can resting on a cork coaster. "I definitely have a plan," he finally said, "but I don't know that I should tell you what it is. It's six o'clock right now. Time for dinner. Why don't you go with Rose, grab some grub at the Quarry Pit, and just stay inside for the night. We'll handle the rest."

I glanced at the clock. It was 6:05. When you're counting down to your own death, every minute is important. I returned to my seat. "I'm not going to do that. You need me."

"Why would I need you? You've already told me where the monster is, and that it can't come out until the sun sets. I have a whole crew of deputies with a reasonably strong arsenal of weaponry. It'll be like scooping fish outta that tank out there with a net."

"I can see into his lair. Maybe I can give you a heads-up on his movements. Stuff like that." I had to admit it felt like a weak argument to me, but it was all I had in the moment. Still, he must have been more nervous about it than he was letting on because he gave in almost at once.

"Okay."

"Okay, what?"

"Okay, I'll let you come with us."

"Come with you and do what? What're you

planning?"

He rubbed his face, took another sip, and glanced up at the clock again. "We can't just go in, but that doesn't mean we can't be ready and waiting when the thing comes out. We're going to surround the place and take it down as it exits."

Flabbergasted was the word that came to mind. I wasn't even sure I was using that word correctly, but I was flabbergasted. It was my turn to rub my face. "I told you that it's the sun that makes him weak. If you wait until he comes out after the sun sets, you lose your advantage."

"It's the best I can do."

"Can't you get a warrant or something? You can't wait for the sun to go down. I'm dead serious."

Anders dismissed me with a wave. "Come if you want. Stay away if you want. Your call. We're headed up there at 8:30. Meet me here at 8:25 to hitch a ride. Until then, go with Rose. Have some fun. Get something to eat. And for the love of all that's good in this little town, stay out of trouble."

Eleven

Journal Excerpts

Judy Steinkamp has a threatening demeanor toward inmates,

but I'm sensing it's all for show. She's sweet on the inside. I like her.

Rose came to rescue me from jail.

The sheriff has a plan but it's risky, very risky. He's going to let me come along. I'm anxious, excited, and terrified, all at the same time.

— • ● • —

Rose offered to make me dinner, but after the lunch we'd had, I suggested we follow the sheriff's idea and have dinner at the Quarry Pit. She hooked her arm through mine and led me into the diner. I don't remember high school, but I imagined the feeling was like a kid who'd lucked into a date to the prom with the prettiest girl in the school.

For its part, the shiny aluminum siding of the Quarry Pit reflected the evening sun sinking in the western sky. I hoped the dinner menu options were as tasty as the breakfast turned out to be. I could almost taste those eggs. They were still within my twenty-four-hour memory window so I could vividly recall every delicious morsel. We took the same corner booth the sheriff and I'd sat in that morning. I sat in the corner itself, so I could see out the front and side windows while taking in the restaurant's ambiance. Rose sat directly across from me with her back to the other diners, smiling sweetly, seemingly oblivious to my inner anxiousness.

"Hey, Rose," the waitress said as she approached with two oversized, plastic, laminated menus. "Is this the famous Doc Moon I've been hearing about all evening? The one who solved old Jasper's mystery?"

This waitress was old enough to have known Jasper Fresno. Her grayish white curls formed a dome above her ears, and her pink lipstick provided a pleasant, muted contrast. The matching pink nail polish completed the package. Looking at her eyes and the shape of her nose, I guessed she could be a sister to the librarian.

"That's him," Rose answered. "In the flesh." She winked at me. I blushed.

The server placed one of the huge menus in front of me. It took up half the table. "Well, sweetie, you've done a good thing there. Old Jasper was a loner. He could be grouchy, and he didn't have many friends, but he was always good to me."

I glanced out the window at the junkyard fence. Jasper's ghost no longer stared back. I hoped he was now able to rest. The two goons were closing shop and locking the gate for the day. I figured they'd taken charge when their boss and his boy fled.

The waitress was still standing at our table, waiting for me to respond. I smiled at her. "I'm just glad I could help," I said, trying to look meek.

"I'll give you two a couple minutes to look over the menu and decide. Be back in a jiffy." She walked down the aisle in front of the counter and stopped at a table in the opposing corner, pad in hand. She wasn't very tall. Her pink diner's uniform skirt dropped well below her knees.

"That's Martha Rae," Rose explained. "She was Jasper's neighbor and about the only person he could call a friend, and even that was a stretch. Fun fact, she has a twin sister who runs the local library."

I'd guessed right again. I nodded and softly smiled, but my mind had moved on from Jasper Fresno. That problem was solved. Now, my brain was completely consumed with the larger issue of how to keep this entire town from dying a bloody, gory death tonight. Well, except for that part that was consumed by the woman sitting across from me. The story of Fresno was a closed book to me, if not to everyone else.

I didn't have much confidence in Anders' plan. Without the sun to weaken the creature, I had my doubts that a barrage of bullets would bring it down. Maybe they would; maybe they wouldn't. Then again, I didn't really know if the sun would do the trick either. Maybe it wasn't as deadly to him as vampire lore indicated. Could be he simply didn't like the sun, or it just made him itch. An image of him using his taloned fingers to scratch up under his cape flooded my mind, then quickly dissipated.

"Do you think it's really a vampire?"

Rose's voice pulled me out of my thoughts. "What?"

"A vampire. Do you think that's what it is?"

How I acquired a thorough understanding of vampire lore, I'm not sure. I seemed to know more than the little I learned in my web searches earlier. I didn't recall watching any vampire movies. Somehow, though, I understood the concept. "I can't know with one hundred-percent certainty, but that's the conclusion I've come to. After all, it only comes out at night, it nourishes itself with human blood, and it has a mouth full of sharp teeth. When I saw it in my visions, I had only glimpses of its face."

"Know whatcha want?" Martha Rae was back at our table. She placed some glasses of water in front of us, then stood there, tapping her red pen on her light green pad.

Rose ordered first. "Country fried steak and gravy. Corn…and…some green beans."

"Drink?"

"Sweet tea, please."

"Got it. How 'bout you, sweetie?" Her bright gaze shifted to me.

I hadn't even glanced at the giant plastic plane wing with words and pictures resting on the table in front of me. It was a huge menu. To move things along, I ordered the first thing my eyes fell on. "I'll take the chicken livers, mashed potatoes with white gravy, and some navy beans." Rose scrunched up her nose. "Give me a Mountain Dew to drink."

"Coming right up," Martha Rae said as she hurried off to give the order to the guy in the back.

I could see the cook through the little rectangular window behind the counter. He wasn't the same guy that made my eggs. This guy was a lot younger. Sharp features. His alert eyes scanned the dinner crowd even as he processed their orders.

I threw my arms up on the back of the red padded seat, took a deep breath, and exhaled slowly, hoping some of my anxiety would seep out with the air. It helped a little. The clock hanging high on the wall above the cook's window read 6:20, and I could hear the time ticking away toward midnight.

"You're going to need some mints," Rose snarked.

"Huh?"

"Your breath is going to be awful after eating that

chicken liver. Not to mention what those navy beans will do to you later."

"Do liver, potatoes, and beans make your breath stink? I didn't know that. I'm sorry."

"Good thing I have access to the best stuff." She pulled a small metal box out of her purse—peppermint breath mints.

I looked for the waitress, but it was probably too late to change the order now. Besides, Martha Rae was on the other side of the diner delivering someone's burger and fries. Bad breath was the least of my worries, but I suppose Rose had something else in mind.

As I gazed at Rose, I examined her freckles, her green eyes, and her complexion. I couldn't help but think that she should have red hair. Instead, her hair was brown with just a hint of red. It was another thought from deep in my psyche, since I had no recollection of ever meeting anyone with bright red hair, freckles, and green eyes before 6:20 p.m. yesterday. Still, the flowing brown tresses looked good on her. Real good.

My attraction to her made sense to me, but if she really was as old as I'd been told, why in the world was she apparently so attracted to me? She'd said she was lonely, and that I *saw* her despite the barrier the ghosts in her house put around her. Maybe that was all there was to it. Two kindred spirits.

My mind was a conflicted mess. On the one hand, I was extremely attracted to this young-looking woman who apparently was nearly twice my age. Rose's reciprocated attraction further stoked the fires. On the other hand, the day was edging toward sunset and the emerging of a vampire hellbent on seeking me out. Not to mention midnight and my envisioned bloody death.

"Rose, do you really think the psychic barrier around your house would be strong enough to block out an undead monster?" It was a question she couldn't answer unless she'd had previous experience with vampires in Cutters Notch. "Never mind. That's an impossible question." My hands were resting on the table, visibly shaking despite my effort at self-control.

Rose reached out and grabbed them much like I'd grabbed hers in the conference room. It sent sparks of energy up my arms as if I'd touched a live wire.

"You're right," she said. "I've no way to know for sure, but I've never known it to fail any other time. The energy the ghosts create has a long range. Ask anyone in town, and no one will even know the place is there. That house only lets in who it wants to let in. Period."

Martha Rae brought the drinks.

Rose looked at me and winked. "Martha, you've known me all my life. Do you know where I live?"

"Hmm. Seems like I ought to. I know where everyone else in town lives…but, no, I don't think I remember." Then she took a long look at Rose holding my hands, pursed her lips, and walked away. I pulled my hands free to put the straw in my soda. "I don't think Martha Rae approves of you holding my hands."

"Oh, who cares what she thinks? The old prude." Rose was smiling at me with some severely kissable lips. Between the monster, the ghosts, and this beauty, Cutters Notch was doing a number on me.

"Oh, look! It's Moon-boy."

The gravelly voice jerked my mind away from Rose's mouth. Over her shoulder I saw that the two goons had come to join us for dinner, stained t-shirts, dirty jeans, and all. No crowbars, though. That was a plus.

"Hey Moonie, got yourself a date?" The other one joined his buddy in the harassment.

The various patrons in the diner dropped their forks and turned to watch the spectacle. The people on the counter stools turned around, and the other folks stretched their necks to see from their respective booths.

The two buffoons took stools at the counter, then spun themselves around so they could continue to throw their verbal hand grenades. "You probably cost us our jobs today, Moon-boy. You got any money to tide us over?" He sounded like the school bully trying to take my lunch money. "The least you could do is buy our dinner."

It seems I have a bit of an impulse-control problem. The wise thing would have been to sit there until they grew tired of messing with me or ran out of creative banter, something that likely would have happened very quickly. I just couldn't do it. They stepped on my last nerve when they started in on Rose. So much for staying out of trouble.

"Hey Rosey, you're pickin' 'em kind of young these days, aren't ya?" asked the one on the left.

"Yeah, Rosebud, I'm available, too. I'll show you a good time. I'll make you bloom like a flower on a spring morning." said the one on the right.

I was a tad impressed with the eloquence of that last phrase, but I'd heard enough. As I stood, I answered them with as much sass as I could muster. "Why don't you two brain-dead zombies get outta here and go find your buddy, Ronnie. He's more your speed. Then you can get a little plastic bucket and shovel to go play in a sandbox somewhere else like good little boys. Rose is a grown woman. You're a couple of kindergarteners. As for me—*the moon-boy*—you don't want too much of my attention. I'll break your teeth and there'll be a lot of soup and pudding in your future."

Perhaps it was a little cheesy, but I thought it sounded tough.

Rose stood with me, blocking my path, restraining me with her hands on my shoulders. I tried to edge past her, but she sidled left, then back to the right, continuing to run interference. Behind her, the two buff-goons stood to meet me. Yeah, I ran goons and buffoons together. It seemed fitting.

I smiled at Rose. "I've got this," I said. She shook her head and refused to move, so I grabbed both her elbows and lifted her in the air. Seemed I was stronger than I looked. Her eyes were as big as fifty-cent pieces. After making a 180-degree turn, I lowered her back to the floor. "I've got this," I repeated.

Smiling again, I turned back to face the junkyard dogs. Humans weren't nearly as scary as vampires. Not to me, anyway.

They wanted to do a little prancing before they started the big dance, puffing out their chests and looking down their noses at me—flexing their fingers in and out. Throwing their elbows outward to try and make themselves look larger. They really didn't need to do that; they already looked huge. Somehow, though, I knew I could take them down.

Through the crack that was the space in between their triceps as they postured side-by-side, I saw the cook come around the end of the counter behind them. He was their age and in their weight class. Curly brown hair stuck out under the white cap he wore. He had a military-inspired tattoo on one arm. In his left hand, he carried a very large chef's knife. As he approached, he seemed to realize he still had the blade in his hand and paused to place it on the lunch counter.

"All right, Razor," the cook said. "And you, too, Blade. That's enough. No food here for you tonight. Just get on outta here. You can go eat at home."

"Really? Those are your names?" I had to ask. The irony was too much. "As dull as you are?" Obviously, I couldn't leave well enough alone, and the sarcasm was irresistible.

Maybe if I'd not said that last little insult and

allowed the cook to throw them out, no one would've gotten hurt. I would've gone back to my Mountain Dew and my feast of chicken livers, and they would've gone home to some bowls of Cap'n Crunch. However, despite their derelict intellect, they understood that I'd just called them stupid and had to prove me right.

Blade and Razor lunged toward me in the same moment, getting in each other's way like two puppies headed for the same dinner bowl. In response, I flung both my hands out like skin-covered pistons and struck each one in the throat, hard. While they grabbed at their necks and tried to gasp for breath, I crouched and punched, my two fists extending together again like two hydraulic hammers. You guessed it. Right in the nuts.

The cook didn't give them time to recover. Instead, while I backed up against the lunch counter and the other diners looked on, he grabbed their shirt collars and escorted them to the parking lot.

It was three big men trying to angle through the same set of double glass doors at the same time, so it took a minute. Since everyone else was distracted, I casually pilfered what turned out to be a truly sharp chef's knife from the countertop. Quickly, I slipped it into my orange jail pants. Don't judge me—I only borrowed it. I figured if I was going to be facing a bloody death in a few hours, it wouldn't hurt to have a weapon to defend myself.

"Go home," the cook said as he pointed away from the Quarry Pit. His voice boomed so loud that we could hear him through the plate-glass windows. The two buff-goons left, but not before spraying him with a shower of curse words. I strolled past Rose, returned to my seat, and sat down. Rose paused a moment, then did the same.

"That was amazing," she remarked. "I thought you were going to get pounded into the shiny linoleum floor.

Where'd you learn to move like that?"

Before I could answer, the cook reentered. "Doc, your dinner will be ready in a couple minutes." Seemed everyone in town knew my name now. That didn't seem fair since I'd only learned it myself that morning.

"Thanks," I said with a wave. My eyes returned to Rose, my mind to her question. Where *did* I learn to do that? I had no idea. It felt like instinct. Or was it muscle memory?

An image sprinted through my mind. A white room with bright lights overhead. A red, matted floor. Large punching bags hung from steel chains. My hands, covered in gloves, were punching a bag so quickly they were a blur. As fast as the image came, it fled even faster and was gone. I was sure now. It was muscle memory, but from what? I'd been trained. When? Where? And by whom?

"Did you take karate lessons or something?"

"I honestly don't remember. Maybe. My long-term memory is toast. Some sort of amnesia. I don't remember anything beyond twenty-four hours ago."

Martha brought our dinners. Gazing at my fried livers and the mashed potatoes with the white gravy oozing over the sides, a sense of warmth swept over me. Using my fork, I swirled some gravy with the mashed potatoes and tasted the delicious comfort food. Surely, I'd had it before, but it seemed like the first time.

I knew from reading my journal that the visions of my future demise were changeable. Since I was obviously still existing, the previous dangers hadn't spelled my end. Maybe I'd make it through this one, too, but that was yet to be seen. My nerves were calm now, my hands steady. Whether it was the gravy or punching Razor and Blade in their respective throats, I didn't know.

I glanced again at the clock over the cook's

rectangular window. The second hand seemed to be spinning around the face faster than it should. Midnight was marching my way, not to mention the sunset confrontation in less than three hours.

I let a few minutes pass, then I carefully slipped the pilfered knife into my backpack. It was sharp, all right. Sharp enough to slice into the waistband of my fancy jail trousers. Rose was too engrossed in her chicken-fried steak to notice. The cook was banging things around in the kitchen, looking for his missing blade. I felt bad for him, but I needed it more than he did.

We sat quietly and ate our respective dinners for the next fifteen minutes. I learned that I actually like fried chicken livers. Imagine that. When I finished the last morsel by swiping a tiny bit of gravy with my right index finger, my eyes returned to Rose and her luscious lips. Her emerald eyes were already peering at me, waiting for me to finish.

The sheriff had told me she was forty years old, but that didn't seem possible. She didn't look a day over twenty-six or maybe twenty-eight on the outside. A tad older than me, maybe, but not that much older. No wrinkles at the corners of her eyes, and her fingers were smooth and youthful. There were no age indicators anywhere.

"Doc, I was thinking," she said, her eyes sparkling. "There's a lot happening tonight, but we've got about an hour and a half before you need to head back to the station. What if we—" She paused, smiling, again taking my hands. Her palms were warm against the skin of my fingers. "We could go back to my place."

Whew, buddy! The look she gave me. I can't describe all the electricity that shot through my brain in that moment. I may be young and have a worthless memory, but I knew what she was suggesting. A beautiful—gorgeous—apparently older woman wanted to take me home, and I was absolutely sure it wasn't to watch TV or play video games. I didn't know if I was twenty or twenty-five, but I was sure that every part of me wanted to take her up on the suggestion, whether she was twenty-eight or forty.

Then, my unfortunately sharp short-term memory flashed the images of our lunch in that same house with thirty ghosts looking on. Two of them were very angry—one of the two stuck her hands inside Rose's brain, making her talk like a puppet. I saw the little girl ghost shove one of the angry ones through a wall. Nope. I couldn't do it. No matter how hot Rose looked as she gazed at me from across the Quarry Pit table, I couldn't imagine making out with her under the watchful, ghostly eyes of her never-ending houseguests.

Still, I didn't want to hurt her, so I couldn't bring myself to tell her no. Also, I just didn't want to say no. The word "conflicted" understates the war raging in my brain in that moment. The answer I hurriedly came up with was a diversion. I needed to find a way to deflect the idea until we were out of time, or we found a reasonable alternative location. Her suggestion was incredibly tempting. A huge battle began between my physical interest and my mental aversion to being watched by apparitions. I had to fight the temptation; I had to stay focused on the dangers coming my way in the next few hours. As much as I wanted to say yes, I had to say no…or maybe…or later.

As the debate raged in my mind, I remained silent. I studied the angle of her jaw, the soft form of her nose, the bright shine of her eyes, and the fullness of her moist lips. My eyes drifted to the curls of her reddish-brown hair as they flowed to her shoulders, framing her neckline to the collar of her blouse, where it, in turn, angled further downward to the top button. I was lost.

"We need to go back to the station," I blurted out as I jerked my eyes back to meet hers.

"Why?" She cocked her head, her expression pleading.

I pointed at my orange jail pants. "I want my own clothes back. They should be dry by now. These things are itchy." That last part was a bit of a fib. The pants were comfortable enough.

"Well, hurry up then, lover boy. No time to waste." She stood and pulled me out of my seat, dragging me to the cash register by one arm. "I'll buy dinner," she said as she pulled her wallet from her purse. "You can cover dessert." Then she winked. I was still blushing when she pulled me outside.

Twelve

Journal Excerpts

The Quarry Pit has incredible food. I like fried chicken livers. Good to know.

The goons from the junkyard insulted Rose at the diner, but I faced them down before the cook ran them off. I seem to have been trained in fighting skills, but by whom, when, and why?

Rose wants more than friendship. I'm so awestruck by her I can hardly believe it. But is she really forty years old or not? And making out with her in front of thirty ghosts puts a little chill on my hot blood.

Rose parked out front, and we walked into the sheriff's office through the visitor's entrance. The place was starting to feel like home, so I circled the counter without being invited. Rose took a seat in the lobby, clearly avoiding any unnecessary chit chat.

"Hey Gator," I said as I entered. "Where's Ms. Steinkamp?" He was seated at a desk in the middle of the main office. A couple other deputies were hanging around the door to the sheriff's personal office. Anders' voice drifted out.

"Gone for the day. Her shift's over. She's coming back after dinner though, to man the station during our arrest on the bluff."

Arrest? Did he really see this as an arrest? Did no one understand how dangerous this was going to be? The sheriff and his team were underestimating the danger, or maybe they were overestimating their own skill. Regardless, I'd done about all I could to warn them.

"She had my pants in the laundry," I explained.

"So soon? I just washed 'em last night. What happened?" He stood, grinning. Gator knew exactly what had happened. By now they all knew what happened. He just wanted to see my face when I answered. I glared at him, refusing to play along.

"Fine," he finally said. "They're folded up, nice and neat and waiting for you on top of the dryer." He pointed, as if I didn't already know where the appliance was located. "Help yourself."

I headed that way, but when I'd moved out of Rose's line of sight, I turned back and motioned for Gator to follow me. When he started to react, I placed a finger to my lips, hoping he'd understand and go along with it.

He caught my drift because he stood, casually laid a paper on Judy's desk, and followed my tracks to the laundry room.

My cargo pants were just where he'd said they'd be, but I waited for Gator to join me before gathering them up. Once he'd walked inside, I closed the door behind him. I needed some straight-up information.

"Gator," I whispered, "how old is Rose? For real. No jokes."

He smiled. "Getting weird for you, is it?" He didn't whisper. "She's obviously sweet on you."

"Come on. Just tell me," I urged, motioning for him to keep his voice low.

"She's older than she looks but not as old as she is."

What kind of crazy statement was that? It made absolutely no sense. I played it over again in my head. *She's older than she looks but not as old as she is.* I was more confused than when I started out. "Could you be a little less cryptic?" I didn't know how patient I was normally, but I lost whatever measure of patience I had in that moment. "That sounds like nonsense. Is it some sort of riddle?"

"She's right at forty. I'm a little older than her, but not by much. A year, maybe two. We went to elementary school together." Gator's ever-present smirk was absent, and in that moment, he was looking me straight in the eyes without a hint of humor.

"How is that possible? She doesn't look like she's even close to thirty?"

"Like I said, she's not as old as she is."

"What does that even mean?"

"Look, she has her secrets. I know some of them, but it's up to her to tell 'em. Why are you so worried about how old she is?" His head was cocked to one side. He'd started smirking again, but the question came out with a genuine tone.

"Have you ever been to her house?" I was going to tell him, but not until I'd received a couple more answers.

Gator gazed off into the corner, thinking. Turning toward the door, he scratched his head before turning back. "You know, I don't know where she lives." It was like where she called home had never occurred to him before. "Weird. In my job, I know where everyone lives. Seems like I should know, but there's a blank spot in my memory."

I understood how that felt.

That house, or more accurately, the ghosts inhabiting it wielded considerable otherworldly power across the whole little town. Rose had said the house only let in those it wanted and blocked everyone else. It seemed even an entrenched resident like Gator was completely blind to the presence of the huge Victorian structure.

"I was there at lunch, and it's a weird old place. Creepy."

"Really? Where is it? Which road is it on?"

My turn to smile. He really wanted to know. "It's on the main drag. Sits right up against the cliff wall across from the General."

"No way!" Confusion spread over his face like a layer of makeup. He couldn't place it, leaving him perplexed. After a moment, he stopped trying as if he'd forgotten the question. The issue seemed to dissipate like my memories after twenty-four hours.

Following a couple seconds' pause, Gator blinked, his face scrunched. A mental reset. "What were we talking about?"

"Rose wants me to go back to her place with her, and…and…" My face and neck warmed. I must have been glowing like a red traffic light because Gator noticed.

"Well damn, Doc, look how red your face is." He placed his hand on my shoulder. "No rose comes without a few thorns," he said with a wink. "Pun intended, but she's about the brightest flower in these parts. I used to chase her some myself before me and Rhonda got together. So, it feels a little weird. So what? You gonna let that stop you? Like I said, she's not as old as she is."

Gator had obviously never seen a room full of thirty ghosts or had a couple of them stick their fingers inside his hostess's brain. He hadn't heard the ghost voices coming out of Rose's mouth. I couldn't explain my feelings about Rose and her place in a way that Gator would understand, so I snatched up the trousers and headed to the men's room to change. A roll of duct tape was lying there on a utility cabinet next to my gear, so I grabbed it along with my backpack. Luck was on my side—for the moment.

Five minutes later, safely back in my own pants with the pilfered knife taped to my thigh, I leaned my head against the bathroom wall and took a deep breath. The pressure of everything I'd experienced since my vision of the previous night weighed on me. Ronnie and his girl. Jasper Fresno. The missing truck driver's death. Stealing the baseball. Seeing the monster. Seeing Fresno's death. Knowing I was up against two deadlines—the creature's sunset confrontation and my own impending death at midnight. One would think some personal time with a beautiful woman would be a welcome diversion, but no, it just added to the pressure I was feeling.

I clicked off the light and kept my forehead against the wall a while longer, my mind drifting across the various experiences of the day. Somewhere in the room, a clock was ticking. I felt every single tick like a jab in my side.

Taking another deep breath, I focused on the immediate danger—the vampire in its lair on the top of the bluff. I concentrated, intentionally doing what I had done by accident earlier. After a moment, my mind lifted above the sheriff's office, then above the treetops. My mind's eye blocked everything else out as it cruised up the side of the rough, stone cliff. This journey was like one of my visions, but those happened to me without my active participation. This one was my own doing.

I rose above the edge of the cliff and continued into the air, drifting eastward toward the old house until I found myself hovering over the garage. The structure on top resembled a miniature tower with six sides, each one with a glassless window.

Downward I drifted, passing through the roofline, through the attic. I saw crisscrossing steps leading to the tower. On a small landing sat a rolled-up rug. Feet wearing large sneakers hung out of one end—the missing boy, Jason. Downward, still further, I passed into the main space and through the ceiling of the cargo container.

There he was, reclining on a bed of sorts, lying on his back, candles all around, eyes closed. I circled above him, taking a closer look, my presence yet undetected. His mouth was open; sharp teeth pointed jaggedly across his gaping maw. His cape was off, and he rested in a white, ruffled shirt and black, shiny trousers. Gray skin covered his feet, and elongated toes with pointed nails extended like blood-red talons.

Taking the opportunity to look around, I scanned the rest of the enclosed space. Candles flickered and popped, lighting the room. An ornate desk rested against one wall. Metal L-brackets affixed the furniture to the floor.

An image hung between candles above the desk— a woman dressed in Victorian-era clothing with her hair done in a winding updo. She smiled with pert pink lips, her complexion pale. A French name adorned the lower right corner.

The floor was covered with dirt, or more specifically, soil. Tracks led to a back corner where I spotted two figures shackled to the rear wall—young girls, the missing teens. Their skin was pale, and they didn't move. The fact that they were still shackled rather than rolled up in rugs hinted that they may still be alive, but I couldn't tell for sure. Empty plastic water bottles and granola wrappers lay scattered at their feet. *How does the monster get the food and water?* The girls were fully clothed, but bloodstains covered their shirts from the neck down. If they were alive, it wouldn't be for long.

I floated back for another look at the creature himself. His form intrigued me. He seemed largely human, but his nose and mouth were slightly extended. With his pointy teeth and angular ears, he had the distinct look of a predatory animal. I couldn't place it, but there was an image in the back of my mind of some sort of flying animal with teeth like that, maybe a bat.

I dropped closer until I was only a few inches above him, examining his taut, gray skin. It looked like stretched rubber pulled onto a skeletal frame, translucent enough that I could see bone and muscle underneath. Blue veins ran here and there, tiny tubes of vampire blood keeping the creature alive.

His yellow eyes popped open, and he roared, thrusting his palms upward. His psychic energy flung me away. This time, I'd scared him almost as much as he scared me.

I passed backward through the ceiling of the shipping container and found myself immediately back in the men's room. The lights bloomed to life and Gator was there. I stumbled backward and he caught me, keeping me on my feet.

"Are you okay?" he asked. "What're you doing in the dark?"

"I'm okay." My heart was racing. The light was slamming into my eyes like tiny needles. I patted the front of my pants to make sure they were dry.

"Are you sure? You've been in here a while, and you just screamed. That's why I came in. What's going on?"

"I was back in his lair," I blurted. "This time, I went there on my own. He has those missing girls in there. They're chained to a back wall. I can't tell if they're alive or dead, but they're still chained up, so I'm hoping they're alive. The missing boy, Jason—I think he's dead, rolled up in a rug near the attic. I never found the Kurz guy. The monster saw me and shoved my mind out just as you came in and turned on the lights—"

My knees buckled. Gator caught me yet again and held me upright.

"Look, why don't you come back out here and sit down for a minute. Catch your breath." He wrapped an arm around my shoulders and led me back to the office.

Rose was standing when I walked into the room, still unsteady on my feet. I sat next to Gator's desk, and she crouched beside me. "What happened? Are you okay?" Her hands were on my knees. That didn't help matters at all.

"I'm fine," I stuttered. "Had another vision. Shook me up." My hands were shaking. I decided I'd rather face down two buff-goons barehanded than go into that storage container again, vision or no vision. Covering my face with my palms, I forced Rose to back off a little, and rested my elbows where her hands had been.

Gator came to my rescue. "Doc, you'd best lie down for a while. Why don't you go back there and rest on one of the cell beds again?"

"He can come to my house and rest," Rose suggested.

"I think he should rest right now where I can keep an eye on him. Come on now, Doc; I'll help you in there."

Rose's countenance dropped, and my heart went with it, but my shaken state was no act. Having that thing's eyes fly open in my face and feeling the power of his psychic energy fling me away was overwhelming.

Even if I *had* been excited to make out in a haunted house with angry ghosts looking on, I couldn't have done it in that moment. Instead, I hobbled under Gator's support down the hall to my bunk. I was beginning to feel attached to the small bed. Taking off my shoes, I lay back, thankful for clean, dry sheets, and placed my arm over my face. Sleep found me in seconds and thankfully, it was vision free.

I awoke to Gator nudging me. The fading light from the windows outside the cell silhouetted his face. Over his right shoulder, the clock read 8:15 p.m.

"Time to rise and shine. We'll be pulling out in a few minutes to go snag a vampire." He chuckled as if it was something he and his fellow deputies did every day. I doubted whether this little town had ever seen much more than an occasional drunk and a few domestic arguments. Then again, it did have a haunted house sitting right in the middle that no one even seemed to notice. I remembered the sheriff mentioning cannibalistic kidnappers that morning, but then he'd mentioned a bigfoot, so I figured he was being less than sincere.

The rest had done me good. My lightheadedness that followed the visit to the creature's lair had passed. Grabbing my backpack, I followed Gator into the main office. A lot of deputies had gathered around. They were all new to me except for Calvin Churchill. He gave me a friendly nod. Judy Steinkamp was back at her desk. She glanced my way and almost smiled.

Anders stood within the doorframe of his office. Everyone else was gathered around before him in the main office area. The sheriff acknowledged me as I entered the room, then he addressed his team. "As you know, this town has seen its share of strangeness over the years. In fact, we seem to attract it. Every few years, we have a new round of screwballs thrown at us."

There went my theory about nothing of note ever happening in Cutters Notch. Maybe I'd underestimated the town.

Anders pointed to me. "Doc is new here, so he doesn't know our backstory—the crazy messes we've faced, but he has already solved one thirty-year-old mystery." A couple of guys clapped. A female deputy gave me a "way-to-go" and a thumbs-up.

Anders stepped to the middle of the group. "Now, we have a new danger to face. Doc tells me, and I believe him, that there is a monster—human-like, maybe a vampire, with a lair inside a storage container locked in the garage of the abandoned mansion on the bluff. You all know the place. The thing has already abducted two of our teen girls and one of the boys. It apparently tried to get Joanie Baxter last night but missed. The girls may or may not be alive. According to Doc, they're locked in there with him."

When Anders glanced my way, I nodded. I tried to smile, but there was no energy behind it. A chill hit my spine and I wrapped my arms around my chest. The crowd of deputies were hanging onto his every word. As crazy as the story sounded, they were taking it all in like it was the gospel. Like they'd been down this road before.

"This creature only comes out at night as the sun goes down. We know where it's hiding, so we're going up there, and we're going to take it down as it emerges. Check your weapons. You each know your assignments. Stay in pairs. Leave no one alone at any time. Understood?"

There was a unified "yessir," and the team filed

out, some through the front door but most through the rear.

"Doc, you're with me," Anders said, motioning for me to follow him out the back way.

Thirteen
Journal Excerpts

Rose really is about forty years old. Gator confirmed it. He said she has a story, but "it's hers to tell." He can't remember where she lives either.

I sent my mind back to the vampire's lair—a new skill that I need to remember I have. The missing boy is dead, but the girls may be alive.

— • ● • —

I'd been wondering about the logistics of being a recluse vampire in our modern world. As I mentally floated around his cozy little den inside the shipping container, I'd seen candles burning, empty water bottles, and used granola bar wrappers. Where would the modern creature of the night obtain his consumables? How would he buy them? Even if he didn't have abducted teenagers chained to the wall to keep alive, the candles would still need to be replaced. How? Was there a second villain here? Did he have an accomplice that did his shopping? Run his errands? It wasn't as if he could just make a run to the grocery store.

More questions filled my mind. Who set up his business deals? How did he arrange to have the shipping container moved to this remote village in southwestern

Indiana? Who set up the orders to have Dave Kurz pick it up and bring it to Cutters Notch?

Then there was the house itself. How did the monster get access? Did he buy it? How did he manage that? No one had mentioned any word of any other strangers in town. In fact, more than once someone had mentioned I was the only new person around, and I certainly wasn't doing the vampire's shopping.

What about his clothes? He might have some innate supernatural qualities, but likely his duds still got dirty. He didn't have Judy Steinkamp to throw them in the laundry for him.

The logistics of how the vampire operated just didn't add up. I didn't see how it was possible. Where did he get his resources? Where did he keep them? How did he access those resources?

I didn't get all the answers, but many of my questions were answered as we approached the gate in front of the old house. A dark blue delivery van was pulling away, leaving four large boxes on the gravel outside the fence of the empty mansion. It seemed that even terrifying night creatures had access to the internet for online shopping. My guess was a smartphone. I didn't have one, but the murderous monster apparently did. He could order anything he wanted, arrange any business he needed to arrange, do all his banking—all through the technology at his talon tips.

That raised new questions. How did he get a phone and arrange for the service? I decided he had to have living, breathing human beings working somewhere on his behalf. Beyond the logistics of obtaining the device, how did he keep the tiny computer charged? There didn't seem to be electrical power running to the garage. In my mind's eye, I imagined a large, cloaked figure plugging his phone into someone's outdoor outlet for a little charge up while he prowled the streets looking for victims. It seemed as plausible as any other possibility.

The gate was no longer locked—perhaps Gator's doing when he retrieved me from the basement. Several Sheriff's Department vehicle's pulled along the road. Most were brown Ford Crown Vics, but there were a few Ford Explorers. Besides Anders and Gator, there were six more deputies—five men and one woman. Calvin Churchill was among them. I didn't know the other four.

They huddled on the driveway, and Anders reviewed the plan again. They were to stay in pairs—two on each side of the structure. Watch for any sign of movement. If the suspect emerged, they were to order him to the ground. I almost chuckled at the term, *suspect*. All teams would converge on the location. They were to defend themselves with deadly force but only if attacked. It wasn't funny, but I did laugh at that one.

Anders glared at me. "You stay right with me. Don't wander off on your own." He didn't need to worry. I might be strange, but I wasn't crazy. I was more than happy to keep him and his guns between me and the vampire. I didn't know if they'd be effective, but it was worth a try.

Light was angling in from the sun's low position in the western sky, painting the white limestone house a shade of burnt orange. The horizon was a terrifying shade of blood-red. The air was calm, no wind. A sense of anxious anticipation hovered around the deputies as they checked their radios and weapons. No quips. No chatter. They were serious professionals preparing for dangerous work.

Anders gave the go sign, and three groups of two headed away in different directions, each determined to bring the perp down as if he were just another random criminal. Gator, Anders, and I took up a position directly in front of the large garage doors with the man-sized door just to the right. We were about twenty yards back. I could see two deputies, Calvin Churchill and a younger man, with semi-automatic rifles in hand, standing not far from the edge of the cliff. The others were out of sight, but they confirmed by radio once they were in position.

The sky above the garage was growing darker by the second, and the moon made its appearance. The air was still humid and warm. Sweat beads trickled down past my eyes and across my nose. My shirt was sticking to my back.

The vampire's face flashed into my mind, surrounded by candles. I winced and shoved it out of my head. It pounced at my psyche again and again, but I kept shoving it away. Dropping to my knees, I pressed my palms on the sides of my head. I needed to know what the monster was doing, but I didn't want it to have free reign to invade my brain anytime it wanted.

"Doc," Anders said. "What's happening? Are you okay?"

I waved him off, focusing on the battle raging in my head. It was all I could do to keep the vampire out. He was slamming against my mind like a sledgehammer against a metal spike. I refused to let him in, putting a mental barrier firmly in place. The creature rammed his mind against it, again and again, trying to get in.

Eventually, the intrusions relented. Instead, a voice knocked softly, quietly on my mind, one with a European accent. "I know you are near," he said. "I feel you close. Are you waiting for me to arise for the evening? Are you that eager to make my acquaintance?"

Apparently, he sensed me but not the others. Maybe they were like insects to him—inconsequential, ants to be trampled on.

My skin grew clammy. It was nearly ninety

degrees, and yet I felt a chill. "No. I have no interest in meeting you," I replied. "I'm only interested in keeping you from hurting the innocent people of this town." I did my best to stiffen my voice and sound confident. I doubt it worked.

"Innocent?" He laughed. It was a deep-throated cackle. "Are any of them truly innocent? I have been watching you humans for 320 years, and I have yet to find one who was truly innocent."

He did have a point, a weak one, but still a point. "They may not be as pure as freshly fallen snow, but they don't deserve to be chained to a wall and drained dry like living water fountains."

It was out of place, but still it occurred to me in that moment that I could recall what a winter snowfall looked like. A real memory. An actual memory washed across my mind's eye of me standing on a snow-covered hillside, sled in hand, looking over a frozen lake. The name *Prairie Creek Reservoir* came to mind. I had no idea where that was, or if it was even the right name. As I write this, that memory is still present in my mind, hanging there like one lone landscape painting on an otherwise empty wall.

"What does *deserving* have to do with anything?" the vampire asked. "Besides, you all lie, cheat, steal, and kill one another with impunity, yet you would deny me the sustenance I require to exist? I have no babies here, no children. Never would I prey upon the innocent. The ones I take are old enough to be accountable for their actions."

The human mind can concoct rationalizations for any number of atrocities. It should be no surprise to me when a vampire has the same ability. Yet, his logic, flawed as it was, did catch me off guard. "I suppose God has appointed you to be his agent of punishment, judgement, and payback?"

"Oh, no. Nothing so grand as that. I need blood to survive. That is my whole purpose in what I do. I choose to take it from humans because they are the most nourishing to me. I take it from those old enough to have lost the shiny newness of innocence to the rust and corrosion of selfish desires. Along the way, I've learned to enjoy the hunt, much as your kind enjoy sitting in a tree stand, waiting for the perfect buck to come ambling by."

He then changed the conversation, perhaps growing tired of the debate. "You're different from any other human I've encountered. You have abilities. Powers. Awareness. You have mental strength that others do not. I can speak into the mind of an ordinary human, coercing them to do what I want, and they do not even know it is I. You, however, know the difference. You recognized my voice as different from your own. Earlier, you even invaded my home on your own. How did you do that?"

I didn't have an answer, and as it turned out, I was the one growing weary of the conversation. It had been a long day after a short night. This creature struck me as both arrogant and obnoxious. My patience was gone. "To be honest, I don't know, and I don't care. Get out of my head!"

"Fine, but soon the sun will drop below the horizon, and I will find you. I will taste your lifeblood, and you will taste mine. I will bring you into the fold of those who share the power of bloodlust under the light of the moon. Together, we will travel the world, see the wonders, and feast upon the blood of multitudes. Think of it, Doc, you and I, we will pass the days in comfort and enjoy the adventures of the night."

Well, there was something I hadn't anticipated. First, Rose wanted to take me home, now this vampire thing wanted to do a little passionate necking of the bloodletting kind, making me a murderous Robin to his villainous Batman. I didn't have an agenda in life, as far as I knew, but if I created one, becoming a vicious creature of the night wouldn't be on the list. Living off human blood wasn't my cup of tea.

"Spending my days holed up inside a discarded shipping container doesn't exactly scream luxury," I replied. "It'd probably get a little cramped with the two of us in there. I think I'll pass on the offer. Thanks anyway."

"Oh, I have other more permanent abodes. They are scattered around the world—New York, Paris, Morocco—many other places. Beautiful, luxurious homes. You will find them most enjoyable. Think of this container as my tree stand if you will. I'm on a hunting trip, a vacation of sorts. In essence, I'm roughing it." He laughed.

"No offense," I spat back at the creature, "but like I said, I'll pass on the whole blood-tasting thing. You can keep your bloodlust to yourself." Then, I shoved hard against his mental intrusion, pushing the vampire completely out of my mind much as he had shoved me out of his space earlier.

When I opened my eyes, Gator and the sheriff were staring at me. Apparently, I'd had that conversation out loud, my side of it anyway. Anders handed me a bottle of water.

The lawmen helped me to my feet, and I stood between them, albeit a tad unsteady, chugging the liquid. I was sweating it out almost as fast as I drank it down. My hand was unsteady as I held the plastic bottle.

"The sun's almost down," Anders pointed out. "If you're right, he'll be coming out in the next few minutes. Stay behind us."

"Absolutely," I replied. "I'll just stand back here and watch you do your thing." The vampire had a mouth full of teeth, the cops had high-powered rifles, and I had a bottle of water. What else was I going to do?

The last hint of the sun dropped below the forest canopy. The horizon still held a tinge of pink, but the sky above had turned a pale bluish gray. The deputies clicked on the lights that hung below the barrels of their weapons. Anders and Gator did the same. The summer song of the cicadas rose from the nearby trees. We waited. We watched. I shook a little.

There was still no wind. Anxiety rose around us like water in a bathtub. Every scuff of the gravel under our feet sounded like it came from a loudspeaker. I could hear the second hand of Anders' watch as it tick, tick, ticked its way around its face. I could hear my own heart as it pushed my blood upward through my carotid arteries.

Just when I thought I couldn't take it any longer, the smaller man-sized door to the garage eased open. First, it clicked as the lock disengaged, then it creaked on rusty hinges as it slowly swung inward. Gator began to raise his gun with the light under the barrel, but Anders stopped him. "Not yet."

A human form filled the void the door left behind. It took a step out and stopped. It was short. At once I knew it wasn't the vampire, but I couldn't see well enough in the low light to know who it was.

As we watched, another form stepped in behind the first, crowding and pushing through the door. The first form stumbled and fell to the ground. The second tripped over the first, falling also. Together, they formed a pile of arms, legs, and torsos just outside the structure.

"It's the missing girls," I shouted. "He's released them."

What was this? Some sort of prisoner exchange? Did he think he was trading them for me?

"Get 'em, Gator," Anders shouted. "I'll cover you.

Cal, you help him."

Gator rushed forward from his position in front, and Calvin joined him from near the edge of the cliff, lights bouncing as they ran. Anders focused his light and the barrel of his gun squarely at the open door. The Maglite clearly illuminated the space just inside the garage. Nothing else moved there as the deputies bent over the girls.

"They're in bad shape, Rick," Gator said. "We need an ambulance. Quick!"

Anders, apparently not wanting to take his aim away from the door, called over to the deputy that Calvin had left behind as he rushed forward—the one who remained standing alone by the edge of the cliff. "Jerry, call it in. Get the EMTs rolling."

There was no response. "Jerry? Acknowledge," Anders demanded. "We need EMTs here, ASAP."

I peered toward the cliff, and the man stood there in silence with his light still angled downward. The beam bounced on the ground around his feet as if it were just dangling in the air. As I watched, a large form filled the air around and behind Jerry. A slight breeze picked up, and a cape billowed, flapping in the open air beyond the cliff face.

A memory of my earlier mental visit filled my mind, images of soaring in and passing through the roofline. I'd forgotten the small, windowed room on top of the garage. A set of stairs led to it. The body in the rug was stashed on a landing along the way. "The vampire has come out through the tower on the roof," I shouted. "He's got your deputy."

I couldn't believe I'd forgotten the tower. It had been there in my vision, but I'd been so worked up over the last conversation that it had slipped my mind. We had fallen into his trap. It had all been a diversion. His latest mental intrusion and the girls being released were all part of his plan to get the advantage. We were like deer trotting right up to his camouflaged stand.

Rick turned his gun, bathing his deputy in the beam of his flashlight. I later learned he was Jerry Steinkamp, Judy's son, but that fact was yet unknown to me. The man was dangling in the air, feet off the ground, held up by one powerful, claw-handed arm. Another hand wrapped around his face, pulling his head to one side, exposing his neck. Jerry's eyes bugged out, large as quarters. The elongated fingers of the vampire muffled Jerry's screams.

Behind the captured deputy stood the monster with his gray skin, yellow eyes, and large sharp teeth. He was grinning ear to ear.

"The girls were a diversion," I said, stating the obvious.

"Units three and four, converge on the cliff position," Anders said into the mic on his shoulder. "Unit two is compromised."

"You think him compromised?" the vampire asked with a chuckle. "I suppose you are quite correct. This is not exactly the way you'd planned for things to happen, is it? You thought you had me surrounded, that you'd destroy me with your bullets. I've seen your kind before, overconfident in your firepower." The monster bowed his head and sniffed at the deputy's neck before turning and placing an ear against his throat. "I can hear his blood flowing through the artery just below the skin. I can smell it, also. A sweet aroma." A long tongue slipped out, licking the deputy's skin just below his ear.

"Put him down!" Anders ordered. "Release him. Surrender, and you won't be harmed."

Gator and Calvin stood, leaving the weakened girls on the ground, then trained their rifles on the vampire. More deputies appeared from around the back corner of the building.

"I don't believe I will," the vampire said, "and you have no power to make me comply. If you fire, you're just as likely to hit your deputy as you are me. Besides, do you think me a fool? I have no doubt you would open fire as soon as I put this man down." The monster's eyes shifted to me. "However, I will make you an offer, one that could, perhaps, spare your deputy's life." The creature's smile widened. "How about an exchange? Like two sports teams trading players. Send over the young one standing behind you, and I will return your deputy to you unharmed."

As he spoke, the vampire's teeth flashed over Jerry's neck, just nicking the skin. A small trickle of blood formed a line from the wound. "Well, perhaps, not completely unharmed." A vampire tongue slipped out again and wiped up the blood. "Tasty. You should decide quickly before I can no longer resist. Blood fever is draining me of my willpower. Once it takes hold of me, all bets are off."

Maybe I was crazy, but I was about to offer myself up to my envisioned fate when Jerry's hand went to his holster. The vampire was distracted, negotiating with the sheriff—one bony, clawed hand wrapping Jerry's right arm against his body and the other hand over the man's mouth, pushing his head aside. That left Jerry's left arm free. An apparent lefty, Jerry's service pistol hung in a holster at his fingertips. The deputy pulled it, angled it back toward the creature's body, and shot him three times, point-blank in the torso. The shots were loud, resonating in the otherwise silent night air.

An intense fire rose in the vampire's yellow eyes, turning them red. The grin left his thin lips as they curled back to reveal the full measure of his fanged jaws. He roared in anger and pain. Then he bared his teeth wide before burying his face in Jerry's throat. Two seconds later, when the vampire again raised his eyes toward us, a hole remained where Jerry's neck had been. Blood spurted into the air around him, some of it splattering on the monster's face.

"No!" Anders shrieked.

"Oh my God!" cried Gator.

Calvin remained speechless, as did I.

Jerry hung limp and lifeless in the vampire's arms.

Spitting out a hunk of torn human flesh, the vampire's long, forked tongue slipped from his mouth a third time and lapped at the blood oozing from Jerry's neck. "Your man made his own deal, it seems. He traded his life for the boy's. Yet, I'll still have the young one before the night is over. Mark my words." He turned his eyes my way. "I'll be back for you, Doc," hc added. Then he tossed Jerry aside like nothing more than a limp washcloth and flung himself over the cliff, dropping from view.

Fourteen

Journal Excerpts

My worst fears came true. It was an absolute nightmare.

One more citizen of this little town is dead. There could be many more tonight.

The vampire wants me to be his companion. If he has his way, I'll become just like him. I can't do it. I won't do it. It's too late to run.

———•●•———

There is nothing attractive about a vampire, nothing romantic. While I was researching this creature at the Cutters Notch Library, I came across references to books and movies that gave the monster a favorable flair. There was even a children's cereal with a vampire mascot. All nonsense. As the monster stood there in the moonlight baring its teeth, holding Jerry in the moments before it ripped out his throat, a gray-skinned face stretched over a misshapen skull, I knew I was staring at evil spawned by the pits of hell.

If the vampire once was a person, it had lost any characteristic that would qualify it as being human. Whatever or whoever it may have once been, it was now a merciless hunter of human prey. Sure, it spoke with intelligent words and phrases and dressed in human clothes, but it considered humanity nothing more than a food source that it could play with much as a cat plays with a mouse.

The aftermath of Jerry's murder was heartbreaking. Most of us were shocked into silence as his body was tossed aside. In defeat, Sheriff Anders dropped to his knees and released a horrified moaning howl that I can't quite adequately describe. Two deputies emerged from the rear of the garage; one stopped to check their fallen comrade, and the other, gun at the ready, ran to the cliff to see where the vampire had gone.

The stunned sheriff, still in the shock of the moment, couldn't speak. Gator triggered his mic to call for help. "Judy," he said, voice breaking, "we need EMTs at our twenty, stat. Send at least two units." Sitting alone in the office in support of the team's action, she would order the paramedics, not knowing her son had fallen in the line of duty. Later, Gator would be the one to break the news that her Jerry was gone. He would do it with Sheriff Anders standing by in silence.

Gator left Deputy Churchill the duty of tending to the injured teen girls while he checked on Jerry's body. He assessed the situation, saw the condition of the sheriff, and took charge. "Cal, get the girls the help they need. Take care of them. Everyone else, join me over here." He stepped back a few feet to allow for the team to huddle.

The four remaining deputies gathered around him. Sheriff Anders pulled himself together enough to join the group. I stood nearby to listen in, keeping one eye on Calvin, just to be safe.

"We have a monster…"

"A vampire," I interjected. Everyone turned their

eyes to me. I read pain and fear there rather than impatience and irritation. They heard me.

"We have a vampire loose in Cutters Notch tonight," Gator continued. "As you can see, it just took out one of our own. Our comrade and friend, Jerry, is gone. We need to get that bastard."

As he spoke, the sounds of sirens rose from the town below, rising through the trees like mourning wails. Tears leaked from my eyes, and I saw on the faces of the deputies that I was not alone.

"It is our duty to protect this town," Gator continued. "Stay in pairs. No one goes off alone. This may be the single most dangerous thing we've ever faced. Understand?"

I thought that was an interesting statement. It "*may be*" the single most dangerous thing? What else had this strange little town faced? What could even approach the danger of the vampire?

"Yessir," everyone replied.

"Keep your weapons ready. It's down there, and it's out for blood. Literally. Get going. If you see it, kill it. Shoot it down without hesitation. If you think it's dead, shoot it some more."

Moments later, two Crown Vics sped away. Gator, Anders, Churchill, and I were left on the scene. I placed my hand on Anders' shoulder as tears drained from his eyes. He hadn't spoken since Jerry had died. "It's not your fault, Sheriff."

"Rick, we need to call the coroner…." Gator said. "For Jerry."

"How am I going to tell Judy?" Anders went to the ground again, his utility belt rattling against the gravel.

I was stunned. At that point, I still didn't know they were connected. "Wait? What? Jerry and Judy? Are they related?"

"Jerry is her son," Gator explained.

I hadn't realized how much I'd grown attached to Judy Steinkamp with her gruff exterior and menacing threats, but my concern for her ran deep. A wave of grief swept over me, and I nearly joined the sheriff on the gravel. Gator grabbed my shoulder. The grief was followed by a sense of rage I didn't remember ever feeling in the past, which, of course, wasn't saying much. I wanted to find that monster myself and rip him apart.

The first EMT squad pulled up. While Gator directed them to the girls, I left the sheriff and walked to the edge of the cliff overlooking the little town. The sky was clear with only a few clouds drifting in the bright moonlight. I could see thousands of stars. A slight breeze swept up and over the edge around my legs. Below, the lights sparkled through the trees.

Down there, somewhere, was death in a cape. He would be looking to kill and devastate and destroy. I tried to sense his presence. Nothing came. He knew my powers; he was blocking me.

"Doc," Gator called, "come back from there. That thing could be anywhere. We need to stay together."

I wasn't afraid for myself in that moment. My appointment with the vampire was still a couple of hours away. Midnight was racing to meet me. Suddenly, I was eager for it to arrive. The bloody meeting couldn't happen soon enough. Rage can be a powerful motivator.

———•●•———

It took time for the EMTs to triage the injured girls and place them inside the ambulances. Gator phoned the coroner and ordered Jerry's remains to be picked up. He did that without running it through the radio to avoid Judy's inherent questions. Calvin snapped the necessary photos of the scene. Then we traveled the few short miles back to the station in absolute silence. Rather than talk, we each stared through the glass of the various windows, both searching the trees and shrubs for a monster and searching our hearts for something to make sense of the loss. There was nothing but darkness—inside and out.

"I've called in more deputies as backup," Judy announced as we entered. "Do you want me to call the neighboring counties for more help?"

We were already aware of the call-ins. Two members of the backup team had arrived at the mansion to guard the scene until the imminent danger had passed. It made me wonder why the extra staff hadn't been arranged for in advance of the showdown. Perhaps they had been overconfident, as the vampire suggested. Perhaps facing those previous dangers had boosted their collective egos and made them feel invincible. It was a moot point now.

"That's good," Anders mumbled without answering Judy's question. Instead, he marched straight to his office, refusing to face his assistant. Still shaken up, he'd retreated into his own mind for the most part. Going through the motions. Beating himself up. Second-guessing his decisions. I'd been questioning his decisions around the vampire for much of the day, but there was no point in doing it any further.

"Judy," Gator said, "would you come in here with Rick and me for a minute?" With a calm voice and a kind tone, he motioned for Judy to follow him into Anders' office. Gator automatically moved into the leadership role previously held by Anders. Seeing his leader was in distress, he stepped up.

"What? What's going on?" She frowned. "What's happened?" she asked as she stepped past the deputy into the office. Clearly, Judy was intuitive enough to catch an unusual tone in Gator's voice. He shut the door. Moments later, I heard another long, howling moan as Judy Steinkamp learned that her son's life was taken. That he had given the ultimate gift in defense of his community.

I sat in a chair watching fish swim around inside the tank on the far wall, listening to Judy's wails. I cried, too. It was as if her pain were my own. Sobbing, I couldn't sit still. I paced the floor, inspected the fish in the tank, and gazed out the darkened window, all with tears still flowing down my cheeks.

Calvin was in the weapons locker beefing up his armor. I was alone in the office with my thoughts. My short-term memory flashed an image of Rose coming to visit me earlier.

Rose? She lives alone at the base of the cliff.

At that moment, I was standing at the back of the station; I could see my reflected face in the glass of the rear door. Maybe I should have told someone. Maybe I should have gotten some backup. But in the moment, I panicked. I had to check on Rose, so out the door I went. Alone.

The previous evening, I'd walked into Cutters Notch in the dark of night without a care in the world, at least none that I remembered. I'd strolled into town, looking for some scraps of food, a hose for some water, and a place to bed down. Now, in less than twenty-four hours, I had people here. People I cared about. Some were back in that office, distraught and crying. Another was sitting like a duck on a pond, alone in her big old house under the trees. Her home was situated directly below the cliff from which the vampire had leaped.

The moon was high as I ran. It reflected off the tops of the wrecked cars on the other side of the chain-link fence to my right. I rushed past the boarded-up schoolhouse on my left, my eyes scanning the upper windows and the roofline for any sign of movement. The dark shape of the bluff rose up, the lighter sky visible above the line of the cliff, and more darkness below it. Trees. So many trees around here. So many places for a vampire to lurk, just waiting for a hapless young man to trot by.

I could still remember where Rose lived, so it seemed I was still welcomed there by a majority of the ghosts. Randomly, I wondered if they took votes on such things, or if maybe the young girl ghost ran the roost.

The General was dark. Closed. It had to be close to eleven o'clock. Remembering the image of Rose's body resting against the glass doors, I paused at the intersection, Bluff Road going one way, Robbins Creek Road the other. Thankfully, that vision was not fulfilled—at least not yet.

Up ahead, I saw a set of headlights from a car headed my way, the silhouette of a light bar on the car's roof. They were moving slowly, flashing beams of light into the gaps in the trees and in between houses. Patrolling. Looking for the killer.

The road options off the main drag of Highway 257 disappeared into darkness. Nothing moved. The whole town seemed frozen in anticipation of what was inevitably about to occur, an audience on the edge of its seat—or perhaps characters in their own play of mass destruction.

Dropping into the trees so the approaching deputies wouldn't see me, I paused again, long enough to shove my mind outward—probing. I mentally searched for the monster, much the way I'd found it in its lair earlier. My mind scanned the town, the trees, the edges of the cliff, the rooftops, and the yards. *Where are you?*

It was there. I could sense its presence; I just

couldn't pinpoint its location. We were like two negative poles on a magnet, repelling one another.

In the distance, the cruiser lit up and suddenly sped toward me, lights flashing but no siren. I saw a deputy speaking into a mic as the pair whizzed past and then turned left onto Robbins Creek Road. In moments, they were gone, and the town was again quiet.

I proceeded to Rose's driveway. Then, standing at its mouth, I let my mind probe the darkness of the trees around her old Victorian mansion. Above the house. Behind the house. Inside the house. I found her ghosts but no vampire.

The ghosts felt my presence and reacted, mostly with a sense of welcome, but that tinge of malevolence remained—the two angry spirits were still angry. Moments later, I stood on Rose's front porch and rang the doorbell. The sound inside was loud and resounding, not the simple ding-dong of the average chime. I heard footsteps, then Rose swung the door wide. She had changed from her earlier outfit into a set of light beige pajamas with burgundy trim at the wrists and ankles. The buttons matched the trim.

The ornate lamp on a nearby table provided little light, so Rose stood in a shadowed room. Her green eyes leapt out at me from within the shade of her flowing, dark hair. She smiled, curling her slightly open lips upward.

Rose's beauty and the temptation that followed scared me almost as much as the vampire. I didn't know what to do with the feelings surging inside me. She was like a riptide threatening to pull me under while a shark circled nearby.

"Did you even look through the glass to see who it was?" I asked as I stepped inside. "I could've been home invaders, or worse, that creature with the yellow eyes and giant teeth."

She laughed, her long hair dancing on her shoulders. "Home invaders wouldn't have even been able to see the place." She stepped over to flick on another intricate glass lamp on the other side of a broad staircase leading to the second floor. "You know how this works. Someone was at my door, and I knew it had to be you. You're the only one they let in. I even need to pick up my mail at the post office because the mailman can't remember the house is here."

"You're so sure." As I stood in her entryway, I placed my hands on her shoulders and tried to look serious. When I touched her, though, a shock ran into my brain and lit me up like a torch.

"I am. Totally." She smiled at my concern.

"What if the vampire is different? What if it can see through the ghosts' psychic blockade? Maybe that's why I can get in." I was thinking out loud. "Because I have some extrasensory abilities. That vampire is strong. It swatted my mind away like I was a fly."

"You worry too much," she said as she took my hand. Her fingers felt warm and soft inside my own. Leading me into her study, she continued, "I believe in the power of this house. It has stood here for over a hundred and fifty years. I know all its history. It won't let me down."

The study was magnificent with its dark wood paneling and its floor-to-ceiling bookcases. A ladder on wheels hung from the top so the reader could roll it back and forth, reaching the upper shelves. A large fireplace consumed the far wall, surrounded by wood panels, and topped by an ornate oak mantel. The flat screen TV mounted above the fireplace seemed too modern for the space—It was lit up with some national news channel. I envisioned a huge portrait hanging there in the past, perhaps some majestic woman or man in nineteenth-century clothing.

A pillowy, leather sofa sat in the middle of the room facing the television and the fireplace. It rested on a large, patterned rug. Lamps flanked the sofa on small tables. Both were lit. Besides a desk and the bookshelves on an opposing wall, the sofa and matching tables were the only furniture in the large space.

Rose sat down and patted the cushion, urging me to join her. I didn't have another seating option unless I wanted to sit at the desk on the other side of the room. "Sit down and tell me what happened. I take it you didn't get that thing when it came out of the garage?"

I considered the prospects of sitting on that sofa next to the attractive woman who'd captured my imagination and aroused thoughts I didn't know I had. Her eyes and smile were inviting. Her lips were soft and moist. Her freckled complexion contrasted nicely with the silky fabric wrapping her frame like a warm embrace. I began to shake with the energy of it all.

It was a difficult decision, one many would perhaps question, but I couldn't afford the distraction. Danger lurked, provided by a vampire with whom I had an imminent appointment. I decided to stay on my feet.

"He got away," I said, "but not before he murdered a deputy." Jerry's gruesome death again flashed across my memories. I couldn't wait for those images to disappear from my mind with all the others. Maybe that's why I'm the way I am. Maybe I've been programed to face incredible danger and then it just slips away from my mind like a misty morning. In that moment, though, I locked eyes with Rose, tears forming in my own. "It was awful, Rose. Just awful."

I was pacing in front of the fireplace. The TV above my head was on mute. The ghosts gathered up behind Rose, forming an audience. They were all there, listening—even the two angry ones.

"Please sit down with me." Rose patted the

cushion again, smiling—this time with compassion rather than flirtation. "Tell me about it. Who did it kill?"

"I'm sorry, Rose. I can't bring myself to describe it. It was vicious and it was gruesome." I paused, staring into the residual ash in the fireplace, trying to contain both my anger and my grief. "Right now, my concern is for you. I hurried here because the vampire jumped off the cliff somewhere above your house."

"You can see I'm fine," she said as the angry male ghost strode to the window as if he were taking up a guard position. "Who did the monster kill?"

"Jerry Steinkamp."

"Oh." Rose's countenance fell like a meteor to Earth. Tears formed in her eyes. "He was such a wonderful man." She stood, walking over to lean on the mantel beside me. "Judy must be devastated."

"She is." I paused. I couldn't think of much else to say. "We did find the missing girls, though," I eventually added. "They're still alive though they're in bad shape, so some good came of it, I suppose."

"Good. That's so good." She tried to form a smile again. It was weak and wouldn't stay in place. "What about Jason? Did you find him, too?"

"We found his remains." I lowered my eyes to my feet and bit my lower lip, trying to control my emotions. Technically, we hadn't explored the garage or the storage container, but I knew where Jason's remains were—rolled up in a rug on a landing heading to the garage attic.

A clock hung on a mahogany wall panel across from the fireplace. I glanced at it over Rose's shoulder. The minute hand was close to the eleven o'clock hour. Whatever was going to happen to me, I didn't want Rose to be there, and I didn't want her to see it. Still, before I walked out of her house, and probably her life forever, I needed to know the truth.

"Rose, did you kill all these people haunting this house? Is that somehow why you don't look much older than me? Gator told me you had secrets, but they were yours to tell."

The angry male ghost turned from the window and rushed back to a position behind the sofa. I could almost see the clock ticking away the time through his opaque body. He was immediately joined by the other irate spirit, the old-looking one with her hair in a bun.

I addressed them next, "Keep your hands out of her head. Let her tell me." They glared at me with eyes burning like street flares.

Rose stepped back from me, stopping in front of the sofa with her hands shaking. "It's a long story, but no, I didn't kill any of them." Pausing, she turned away. "Well, I suppose that's not entirely true." The angry apparitions trailed her. "There are two that could be on me. The others are the victims of one of the ghosts among them. An old woman.

"Minerva Woodstock was well over a hundred years old when I met her, but she didn't look much past seventy. She was going to use me to dial her age clock back again." Rose's hand went to her throat. Her fingers appeared to be searching for something that wasn't there. I'd seen her do that same thing earlier.

"In Minerva's case, I was defending myself," Rose continued. "She tried to kill me, but I fought back and shoved her down those stairs out there. She had this terrible power, linked to a piece of jewelry. It would drain the lifeforce out of others causing her own age to regress. When she died, that power transferred to me, as did the ownership of the crystal necklace that contained it. As old as she was, that event also dialed my life clock back a few years." She circled the sofa followed by a spiritual entourage.

The angry old woman ghost with her hair in a bun

must be Minerva Woodstock. When I glanced at her apparition, she glared back at me.

"I killed a man, too, but again, it was self-defense. I'd had the power for years and never used it. In fact, I'd actually buried the necklace in my backyard for a while before I bought this house. I was terrified that I'd be tempted to take advantage of the power as I aged. When I moved here, I dug it up and the necklace came home. Then, a few years ago, an evil man came to Cutters Notch. I stood back and let the jewel do its work. That dialed my life clock back even more, making me look almost half my actual age."

That explained the angry man. He was also glaring at me.

The little girl ghost stood in front of Rose, nodding to give affirmation to the explanation.

"How? How does the jewel turn back your life clock to make you look fifteen years younger than you are?"

"You wouldn't believe me."

"I'm chasing a freaking vampire. Of course, I'll believe you!"

"Okay. Fine. The truth is I don't really know where the power came from. The crystal had a very long history going back hundreds of years, maybe thousands. I've inherited all the memories of all the owners and victims. However, the earliest memories are strange and hard to understand. Like I said, the woman who owned this house before me, Minerva Woodstock…. Well, she owned it for well over a hundred years. Maybe close to a hundred and fifty. Minerva found the magical necklace when she was a child. First, she let her sister try it on. The girl immediately died."

That would be the powerful little girl ghost who was smiling at me.

"Minerva learned that if put on by someone other

than herself, the jewel would pull that person's lifeforce and transfer it to her. She'd done it many times over her long lifetime. As for me, Minerva lured me here to steal my life so she could be young yet again, but I turned the tables on her. She died, withered away to dust right out there at the base of the stairs. At that point, I took possession of the jewel, or maybe I should say it took possession of me."

"What about the man, the one you killed? What's his story?"

"Al Havener was his name. He was a criminal out for revenge. He tried to kill me, my nephew, and my nephew's friend, but he became enamored with the necklace while he was toying with us. I let him put it on, and it did its thing. My red hair turned more brownish, and I lost several years of aging."

My eyes found the two angry spirits again. Now, they were shooting furious eyes at Rose. Around them circled the other ghosts, glaring at them. It was clear Rose was telling the truth.

"Where's this necklace now? Do you still have it?" I wondered if it could perhaps mesmerize the vampire.

"No. It's gone. It'll never hurt anyone ever again." She smiled. "My age is what it is, now."

The clock on the wall chimed the eleven o'clock hour, pulling me out of the story and back to the present. If my previous night's vision came to reality, I only had one hour to live. One hour to change my fate. If I lingered inside this house, the reality of the bloody vision might follow me. I couldn't do that to Rose.

Rose must have seen me eyeing the door because she moved to stand between me and my exit. "Doc," she said as she wrapped her arms around my waist, "don't go out there. Stay here. Stay with me." Rose pulled me into a full-frontal embrace, pressing her soft body into mine. Her right hand found my neck and pulled my face downward to meet hers. She kissed me and I let her, soaking in the experience. Then I kissed her back. As I did, my body awoke in a way I'd never experienced. She pressed her form against me, and I pressed right back. Our kiss was soft at first, then harder, more urgent. My hands drifted across the silky fabric covering her back even as her hands slipped under my shirt. My fingers found the edge of her pajama top, then the skin of her lower back. Electricity shot through me. I pulled her tighter.

My will to resist was leaking away. I lost all ability to think clearly. Logic was gone. The consequences were immaterial. I wanted this woman. I couldn't help it. The rest of Cutters Notch be damned. My own life be damned.

Just as I was about to lose myself into her spell completely, on the cusp of the point of no return, Rose pulled back, jerking away. Behind her stood the angry male ghost, his eyes like fire. Both his hands were inside Rose's head.

Eyes wide and body stiff, Rose spoke, her voice deeper than seemed possible. "She is mine. She is mine. She is mine." That's all that the apparition said, but he said it through Rose's lips, over and over and over again.

I tried to pull her away, but the spirit hung on her like a cape draping her back. The ghost caused her to stagger, then he lowered her to the sofa. She sat there, eyes closed. Asleep. The dead man's eyes were also closed.

As had happened at lunch, the small female ghost shoved the male apparition aside, albeit with less force than she'd used earlier. Taking the previous ghost's position behind Rose, she slipped her hands into the woman's mind.

Rose's eyes flew open again, and she began to speak in a softer, younger voice. "We will protect her. You need not worry. However, your presence here is causing strife among our number. Most support you, but Minerva and the evil man now reject you, my sister because you know the truth, and the man because he is jealous. Our unity is crucial but tentative. Without it, we cannot maintain our barriers. You must leave. I am sorry."

Behind Rose, the rest of the ghosts formed two lines, facing one another, creating an aisleway leading to the front door. The consensus message was clear. I needed to go. My welcome was revoked.

I took a moment to gaze at her beauty one more time. The shape of her eyes, the freckles on her cheekbones, the softness of her shoulders. I wanted to lock the vision in my memory. I wanted to remember the taste of her lips and the touch of her skin. Yet, I knew in twenty-four hours, it would be gone, forgotten like the rest of my life.

Passing through the gauntlet of apparitions, I paused to peer at each of their semitransparent faces. I wanted them to know that I saw them. They were known. Most had been quite young—teenagers selfishly taken to benefit the old woman. Minerva had been another kind of vampire—one that sustained herself on the lifeforce of others rather than blood, but a vampire, nonetheless.

At the door, I looked back into the room. They all stood there watching me, sad expressions on each face. I felt their sense of loss. The potential of their lives had been stolen. Now all they had was Rose, and they meant to keep her.

Resigned to the outcome of my fate, I exited through the front door. On the porch, I paused to take in the night. A slight breeze rustled the leaves. The moon was still visible through the upper branches. I could smell the sweet musty odor of the forest floor. Somewhere out there was a monster. After trotting down the steps to the driveway, I headed back to town. It was time to track down a vampire.

Fifteen
Journal Excerpts

Empathy sucks, but I wouldn't trade it away.

It hurt so much to hear Judy's devastated wailing and grief,

but it's better than feeling nothing. I couldn't take it if,

in addition to having no memory, I also had no feelings for others.

Rose and I had an intense encounter. She held me, kissed me, and I kissed her back.

My heart yearns for her, but I can't have her.

The spirits that hold her have expelled me. I'm no longer welcome.

———•●•———

Dying at midnight was the last thing I wanted to do. I really wanted to turn around, find a way to rid the house of the ghosts, and claim Rose for myself. Her chronological age was much older than my apparent age, but if what she said was true, her physical age was close enough to mine to satisfy my sense of weirdness. I wanted to experience the passion of her kisses again and again. I wanted to feel her body against mine. Yet, I was certain that if I didn't face the vampire head-on, many other people would die. Maybe Rose, too.

Was the power of the spirits in the house strong enough to keep out the mind of the vampire? Could their barriers withstand, even repel his inexplicable psychic power? I couldn't know for sure. All I could really do in that moment was hope, so I hoped Rose would be safe. Maybe I'd be safe there too, but one thing I did know: If the vampire didn't find me, it would find someone else, and that someone could be Rose. I had to find it first. And I had to find a way to kill it.

The town was so quiet. The frogs were croaking among the trees when I reached the end of the driveway. A bat swooped under the lighted streetlamp near the General Store, snagging his own late-night snacks. I stood just inside the invisible barrier, at least where the barrier was when Ronnie lost us earlier. That felt like a lifetime ago.

The street was empty. Everyone was likely at home, locked up tight. People were already on edge in Cutters Notch and word travels fast in a little town. The news of Jerry's death had probably filtered through the grapevine already. "Stay inside. Lock your doors. Don't open up for anyone. There's a killer loose in town." I could almost hear the conversations.

Eventually though, someone would venture out. There would be curiosity. There would be bravado. Maybe some guy who only smoked in his garage would slip out to light up. Maybe a couple fearless teen boys would crawl out of their bedroom windows, planning to meet up and drink that six-pack they'd pilfered. The monster would have his prey. Human nature leads to recklessness, and recklessness has consequences.

Maybe I was meant to be the sacrifice that would send the monster on its way. It had to know it couldn't stay here any longer. The vampire had probably already arranged for another flatbed truck to pick up the storage container in the morning. It had one night left to create havoc and feast on the blood of this little town. Perhaps, my destiny—shown to me in the vision as I strode into town—was to provide that feast, so the others might live.

I stepped off the driveway onto the sidewalk and let my mind expand. With my eyes closed, I mentally probed around the buildings and into the trees. In crawlspaces and in the treetops. On roofs. Searching. Seeking. *"Where are you?"* I asked.

"Are you ready to join me?" The reply wasn't immediate, but it didn't take long.

Someone screamed in the distance. A woman. The terror she felt reached my mind just after the sound reached my ears. I couldn't tell exactly where she was or who she was, but she was definitely at the other end of town. I could sense the direction.

I cut the mental connection to the vampire and headed toward the park, crossing the road. The streetlamps lined the bluff side of Highway 257, opposite the numerous smaller houses and businesses on the other side of the street.

The rich folks who had lived here when the town was modernized—the ones with the stately homes set back in the trees below the cliff—could probably pay for streetlamps. They lit up their walkways. Those on the working-class side walked in the dark. Not wanting to be easily spotted, I stayed on the poor side of the road.

My intended destination was the same picnic table in the park where I'd sat earlier—a central location. As I walked, I peered between houses, between buildings. Nothing moved. No music, no voices. My only accompaniment were the croaking frogs and the singing cicadas hidden within the surrounding forest.

I approached Ronnie's house. It was dark, but

Pete's house next door was lit up. I stepped in something wet on the sidewalk and paused to examine it. A small pool formed from a dark liquid trickling toward the road from Pete's front steps. Blood. Pete was lying on his porch, half on the steps, his head tilted toward the road. Dead. I didn't need to check to be sure. Dead eyes stared back at me, and his throat was ripped apart; blood continued to drain from his corpse.

I continued past Ronnie's place, remembering my vision of the librarian on the library's front steps. At the time I didn't think that was a premonition. It was too late for the library to be open. Or was it? Maybe they extended their hours since the days were so long in the summer. Maybe she'd stepped outside for a smoke. She could be the woman who'd screamed. I started running, passed the park, and approached the big limestone building.

Sure enough. There she was, sprawled on the steps, the light above the big double doors reflecting off the shiny cord that held her reading glasses around her shredded neck. The red nail polish perfectly matched the blood that soaked her pressed white blouse. Smoke drifted in the wind from a cigarette still smoldering on a nearby step. The woman's eyes were open, empty of life but still full of terror.

"Why?" I screamed into the darkness, trading stealth for speed as I ran out into the open. The vampire had to know where I was at this point. "Do you only kill for sport? Is it fun for you? A game?"

Trees were everywhere in this little town, which rested right up against a national forest. From somewhere in that forest around me, laughter echoed off the face of the cliff across the highway. *"And what a sport it is."* The creature's voice came into my mind in response. *"Agree to join me, and I will end it now."*

"So, I let you taste my blood. You make me one

of your kind. Then, I get to live in a metal box in the dark for eons. Is that about right? Sounds like a life of real joy." I turned, leaving the dead librarian where she lay, and dashed back toward the park. I was too late to help her, and guilt encompassed my heart. Perhaps, if I hadn't squandered time at Rose's place, she'd still be alive.

The vampire hadn't responded to my sarcasm, so I tried to engage him again. I figured if he was talking, he wasn't killing. "Is that the wondrous life you're promising me? Living alone in a metal box in the dark? That wouldn't be too good for my complexion."

"You cannot imagine the power I hold, the abilities I have, and the wealth I have amassed. We would not abide in a metal box. I've told you of my luxurious homes already."

Would I still lack a long-term memory if I became a vampire? Would I wake up in the dark somewhere and not remember what I was? I'd probably step out into the sun during the day, and accidentally fry myself…or evaporate…or whatever happens to vampires in the sun.

"Besides, you would not be alone. We would be companions. Together, we would take what we wanted. Build a kingdom all our own. Enjoy the spoils of the world around us."

The road through town was still quiet. I would have expected deputies to be driving through. Even the cicadas had fallen silent. My eyes searched the shadows, the treetops, the rooftops, any crevice where the creature could lurk. I'd given up the mental probing. He was clearly blocking my ability to locate him that way. I needed to talk him out.

"Yet you're alone. What happened to the vampire that made you?"

"I could include that beauty you're enamored with," he answered, avoiding my question. *"She could*

join us, and we could be a trio."

The monster had been spying on me. It was aware of Rose. My mind's eye created an image of Rose with gray, latex skin stretched over her skull and a mouth full of razor blades. I also remembered that I'd had a vision of her lying dead against the doors of the General, similar to how I'd just seen the librarian on the stone steps. I no longer wished to respond to his prodding. My stomach lurched.

"Where are the patrols?" I whispered to myself. It was a small town. They should have cruised by again. They should have noticed Pete and the librarian lying dead on their respective steps, draining blood onto the sidewalks. Judy said she'd called in other reinforcements. There should be deputies everywhere.

Laughter again echoed over the trees and off the face of the cliff above the town. *"I played the magician. With a little sleight of hand, I've created a distraction to ensure our privacy. They're looking in the wrong place."*

"What have you done?"

"Let's just say I've drawn them away from the center of this cozy little hamlet."

Just as I predicted, the monster was planning to wreak havoc on Cutters Notch in one bloody night. He had already begun. At least three were already dead, and I had no idea what he'd done to draw away the authorities. Time was ticking toward midnight and the moment when I would join the dead. If death was my destiny, I would embrace it. However, I would not be turned into another creature living in the dark, sustaining itself on human prey.

The bloodletting beast fell silent. He no longer cajoled me to join him. With his silence, a thick sense of anxiety swept through town and landed in my heart. He was coming for me. He was coming for me soon. I refused to go to the only place I could possibly hide for fear of leading him there.

Reaching the park, I found my favorite picnic table and sat on its top, my feet on the bench. It was as good a place as any to die. I scanned the ring of houses that framed the small urban forest. A few lights shone here and there, but no one was outside. With the light of the moon and a tiny bit of illumination from a streetlamp across the road, I could see just well enough to write. I pulled out my journal and began to scribble down my final thoughts while I waited for the inevitable.

I could feel him. He was coming.

Sixteen

Journal Excerpts

At least two more are dead.

The creature claims to have great wealth.

He plans to share it with me when I become his companion.

That is something I cannot allow to happen.

———•●•———

Adding my last memories to my journal, I had my head down, but my ears perked. The pen was scribbling words across the lines on the paper as fast as I could make my hand move. It was struggling to keep up with my mind. Thoughts, feelings, and details were spilling onto the page like the torrent of a waterfall.

A twig snapped in the grass behind me. Someone was approaching slowly, silently, like a lion slipping up on an inattentive gazelle. Even as I wrote, I'd kept my mind probing for the vampire. This was not him—not yet. Another hunter was about.

"Hello, Moon-boy."

I turned to see three sets of feet under the dark canopy of the park trees. Two carried the buff-goons and one set held up the son of the local fugitive. As much as I didn't like Ronnie and his buddies, they were in severe danger, and it wasn't from me.

"Fellas, let's not do this tonight. It's not safe out here."

"Yeah," the goon on the right said. Was that Razor or Blade? I couldn't remember which was which. "It's not safe for *you*. We're gonna kick your ass. You've had it coming all day."

Mustering as much compassion for these guys as I could find in my heart, I tried to reason with the unreasonable. "I'm serious. There's a dangerous killer out for blood. He's already killed at least three people." I stood up, positioning myself so the picnic table was between us.

Ronnie ignored my warning. Instead, he stepped up, directly across the wood-slatted tabletop from me. "You ruined my dad's life today," he snarled. "It wasn't enough that you stuck your nose in my business last night. Today, you had to take my dad down."

"Well, he did kill Jasper Fresno." I responded, Ronnie's accusation temporarily distracting me from the danger at hand. "I'd say he sorta ruined that man's life before hiding his body under a pile of tires." I didn't really want to fight these guys although I wasn't afraid of them. I had the skills to deal with them—even three-on-one. Call it instinct. I could take them out, but I had a bigger pie in the oven, one with a timer about to ding.

"That was what? Thirty some years ago?" Ronnie spat out the words through clenched teeth. "You couldn't just leave it alone? My old man's never hurt anyone since. He's run one of the few businesses that employed people around here. After destroying everything he's worked for, you didn't bring Jasper back to life, did you?" Ronnie moved to his right, toward the end of the table. I moved a corresponding distance to my right, keeping the gap between us. That strategy was flawed because the buff-goons were still in their same spots. If I continued around the table, I'd be between Ronnie and his hoodlums. It was beginning to look like an inconvenient fight was inevitable.

"Lucky for you, my dad's not dead, so I'm not gonna kill you, but since you ruined his life, I'm going to ruin yours. I'm gonna mess you up real bad. Eye for an eye."

"Rose won't even recognize you no more," spouted Blade. Maybe it was Razor. Both men were grinning, itching for the action to begin.

"Yeah," the other one added between chuckles. "She won't want no one-eyed, mush-faced boyfriend."

I put my hands up. "Look, I'm sorry, okay? I didn't mean to cause any harm."

Ronnie went around the end. I stood my ground. "I don't care what you *meant* to do. I care about what you did, and you're going to pay. Simple as that."

"What about Joanie?" I asked. "Like I said, there's a vicious killer out tonight. The same one that chased her into her mother's house early this morning. Is she safe? Do you know?" Razor and Blade stepped closer, angling in from the other side.

Ronnie's eyes blazed. He balled his fists, lifting his shoulders and puffing his chest. His arms were bare in a white muscle shirt, his triceps flexed, standing out like hard ocean waves under his skin. "You leave Joanie out of it," he shouted. "She's fine. We just left her at her mother's...right over there." He pointed without looking at a small house through the trees. "The one with the porch light on."

When I glanced that way, a cloaked figure drifted closer in the shadows. He was moving silently, as if carried on the wind. Panic hit me like a brick in the head. The killer was coming, and these guys were too stupid to listen.

The vampire's voice returned to my mind. *"It appears that you need some assistance. Shall I come help you? Yes. I shall rescue you. That is a fine idea."*

"No!" I shouted at the monster. "Stay away."

Ronnie and his buff-goons chuckled. "Go ahead, Moon-boy," Ronnie said. "Beg. Maybe get on your knees and cry out for mercy. I want to see you grovel. Maybe I'll just break your jaw and bust out a few teeth instead of blinding you."

Blade and Razor said nothing. They stood together under a large oak, tapping their respective crowbars in their giant palms. Confident and entertained buff-goons, ignorant of their imminent deaths.

Ronnie stepped forward, grabbing me by the shirt and cocking his right hand back in a fist. I could smell the beer on his breath. He wasn't just stupid; he was drunk. "Nah, beg all you want, but I think I'll ruin your pretty face anyway. I'll smash your nose and take out at least one of your eyes." His clenched teeth morphed into a scary, twisted grin; his fist seemed as big as the top edge of a sledgehammer.

He was about to throw the punch and I was about to react when the goons began to scream like schoolgirls, high-pitched and loud. Ronnie released my shirt. He and I turned in unison to see his buddies hanging in the air, feet dangling, each held aloft by one vampire hand wrapped around each of their necks. Glowing yellow eyes and a toothy grin glimmered between their shoulders.

"You should not have troubled my young friend," the vampire growled at Ronnie.

The victims' hands clawed at their own throats, trying to break the monster's grip. The creature itself stood between them, holding them out like trophy fish. Its gray fingers wrapped around their necks, throttling them as its talons sunk into their skin. Blood oozed from the nail punctures and dribbled down, soaking their t-shirts. Terror flashed from their eyes like bright headlights on a dark country road.

"He may be kind and benevolent, but I am not."

The goons' screaming stopped. They gurgled and gagged, fighting for air, but losing the battle. Their legs swung wildly, kicking and thrusting at the vampire to no effect.

Ronnie didn't move, likely frozen with fear. "What is that?" he sputtered.

"Put them down," I ordered the monster. "Put them down now." I was afraid but I wasn't frozen. I hadn't exactly made peace with my fate, but I intended to face the creature, come what may.

The light from the streetlamps caused the vampire's sharp teeth to shine as its lips again pulled back in a grin. Its yellow unblinking eyes shone in the darkness. "I think not. Not yet anyway." Glancing from one dangling victim to the other, it added, "I like this game."

"Put them down," I ordered again. "It's me you want anyway, right?"

The creature cocked its head and smiled. "Okay. Fine," it replied. Before complying, though, it slammed the heads of the buff-goons together with so much force that the sides of their faces looked like flat tires. Blood broke out and streamed across the monster's fingers. It lapped it up like a thirsty dog. When it finally released them, they fell to the ground like skin bags full of bricks, lifeless dead weight.

Ronnie screamed. His terror echoed across the park beneath the tree canopy, bouncing off the various houses before coming back to our horrified ears. He started to run, but before he could get his feet to move, the vampire was upon him.

"Do you want a taste?" the vampire asked me as it

stood behind my human enemy, wrapping its left arm around the man and pulling Ronnie's head aside with its right just like it'd done with Jerry. The man struggled against the monster's grip, but he couldn't break free. Ronnie's carotid artery pulsated, the blood rushing through to feed his brain.

"Please don't," I begged. "You've killed enough already. Don't do this."

It laughed. "Oh, I have only just begun to kill this evening. I plan to fill these streets with so much blood that a canoe could float from one end of town to the other. I'll paint every white house red. Blood will drip from the streetlamps and streak the windows from your precious sheriff's office down there to the hardware store at the east end of town."

"Please," I pleaded again. "Don't."

"You amaze me, young one. This human has harassed you all day. He threatened you with severe injuries and was ready to make good on that threat. Yet you would beg me for his life? Such integrity." The vampire paused then, studying me. Ronnie's eyes were in a panic, darting from place to place. "Of course, I might stop on one condition." It didn't finish its sentence. Rather, it waited to gauge my curiosity, waited for me to take the bait.

I knew what it was doing, but I responded anyway. "What condition?"

"Join me, and I will relent. Become my companion, and we will leave town before dawn. No one else needs to die. Not here, anyway."

"Why? Why do you want me so bad?" Despite the horrifying prospect of becoming one of the killers of the night, I was curious. I didn't get it. It could have anyone, yet it wanted me.

"Isn't it obvious? I'm lonely. I've grown weary of ravaging humanity all alone. I want a companion, a friend. Someone with whom I can share my adventures."

"But why me in particular?" I was baffled at its interest in me. If it wanted a companion so desperately, why didn't it just turn one of its other victims? Why not Kurz or Jason or one of the girls?

"Because you are different from the others. You have integrity, and you have abilities. We share similar mental powers."

The vampire's sharp fingernails dug into Ronnie's neck, and like with the buff-goons, blood oozed. It caught the attention of the monster. It sniffed, drawing in the iron-laced aroma. "Ah," it sighed. "I can resist no longer."

As I watched in horror, the vampire sunk its shark-like teeth deep into Ronnie's neck and began to pull his blood out in massive gulps. The life literally drained from the man's eyes. There was so much blood flowing that it spurted out between the killer's teeth. At that moment, I considered two things: First, maybe it wasn't my own bloody death I'd seen in the previous night's vision, and second, I could never let myself become a bloodthirsty vampire. I could never be what that thing was.

The night-bound creature was still sucking the last ounces of blood from Ronnie's corpse when my determination to face the beast failed. I grabbed up my backpack and ran. Although I didn't have a destination in mind, I was desperate to get away. Ignoring all the rules, I ran straight down the middle of Highway 257 and headed toward the Sheriff's Office or the General Store or someplace to hide until dawn. Any thought of bravado I might have had disintegrated with Ronnie's jugular.

I hadn't gone fifty feet when Ronnie's head went rolling past me like a bowling ball with a nose. His eyes were wide open, and blood pinwheeled out of what used to be his neck as it went. Running obviously wasn't going to work. Plus, what happened to Ronnie pissed me off, replacing my fear with a resurgence of rage. Ronnie was a punk, no doubt about it. He was the town bully, but as bad as he was, he didn't deserve to die like that.

The deaths of the buff-goons flashed in my mind. They didn't deserve it either. Nor did the librarian, Pete, Jerry Steinkamp, or the kid, Jason. Whatever mayhem the vampire had concocted to draw all the deputies away probably also involved lost lives. This devastation had to end, and if it was going to end, I was going to end it.

The problem was I had no idea how. The vampire was bigger and taller than me, and obviously incredibly strong. Not to mention its teeth and its talon-like nails— formidable deadly weapons—gave it more advantage. As fast as it was, it could catch me whenever it pleased. The fact that I was still running meant I was now its plaything, a new toy for it to push, pull, and twist.

Realizing that running was a waste of time, I stopped in the middle of the road, my back still to the creature, and watched as Ronnie's head came to rest in front of his own house. His empty eyes stared blankly back at me. Pete still lay like a rug on his front steps. At least his blood had stopped flowing.

"You can run if you like," the vampire said, "and you can hide, but I will find you, killing everyone I encounter during the search. I will catch you, and I will have you. Although I do find your sense of right and wrong to be quite entertaining, you will join me, and eventually, you will learn to love our existence together."

I took a deep breath to steel my will and closed my eyes to gather my wits. Then I turned to face the monster and whatever the outcome would be.

The vampire stood in the middle of the road, pausing its pursuit to face me. We were two gunslingers meeting for a shootout at high noon, except there were no guns, and it was high midnight. A streetlight silhouetted it at first, but the creature took a couple strides, and another lamp lit up its hideous face.

"Do you have a name?" I asked. "You seem to know me, but you haven't introduced yourself." I felt the knife from the diner still taped to my leg. It was sharp and dangerous, but how could I even get in position to use it? "You want me to become your companion, but I don't even know who you are." Delay, delay, delay. Perhaps time was my ally.

It stood there as it considered my question. From twenty feet away, the dark cape it wore fluttered in the warm night breeze. The gray skin on its bald head reflected the light from the streetlamp. "You make a fine point, Doc," it said with a grin. Blood caked the monster's cheeks and chin like clown makeup. "Allow me to introduce myself."

Despite myself, I began to feel his humanness again. Whatever remained of the man he had been seeped into my mind—one moment it was a terrifying monster, the next he was a broken, distorted person. My mind was conflicted. Sometimes he was an it—a creature; sometimes it was a he—a person.

He clasped his hands together across his chest. Then, he bowed and followed that with a little dance on the pavement. "People once called me Maurice," he chortled. "I can be a joker. I used to be a smoker. I tried being a midnight toker. I never used to hurt no one. I played music in the light of the sun." He paused, watching for my reaction. "Now, I'm the purveyor of death," he added his own lyrics.

The curled nails at the ends of his elongated toes clicked and clacked on the pavement like taps on the bottom of dance shoes. He seemed so pleased with himself that he laughed and repeated the performance, adding even more lyrics. Then he gave me another courteous bow. The sight was surreal. He stopped his little song and dance. "I love the Steve Miller Band. Don't you? 'The Joker' is a great song." With a glare and with no lyrical quality, he added, "Now I speak of the pompatus of blood."

As it turns out, my invisible memory whiteboard does contain quite an extensive song list. I did recognize the tune he'd stolen and badly butchered, but I wasn't going to give him the satisfaction. "Was that an actual song? Is your song and dance supposed to carry some meaning to me? I'm not really up on popular music," I lied.

The smile faded from his lips. "How could you live and breathe and be as old as you are, and you don't recognize 'The Joker'? I mean, I changed up the words some, took some minor liberties with the lyrics, but it should have still been recognizable. Is my singing voice that bad?"

It seemed a minor point considering everything else, but yes, it was that bad. Even so, it didn't seem prudent to answer his question honestly—or at all.

Maurice glanced up and to the right as if he were reminiscing, reliving some joyous memory. "I had the opportunity to experience that song during a live concert. The Steve Miller Band was on a European tour, and I was perched in the rafters. The music was delicious…and so were the two girls who wandered alone down a hallway, backstage. They screamed, of course, but the music was too loud for anyone to hear."

I began to backpedal. Slowly at first, then faster. The vampire kept pace, continuing to speak as he strode toward me.

"Anyway, I especially enjoyed that song because

my name truly is Maurice. I was born in a country manor in the Picardy region of France around the time the Huguenots were being persecuted. My family was among their number, and we managed to flee to England, no thanks to the French king and his army. It seems like just the other day, though. Time runs together when you're as old as I am. You'll see." He waved the thought aside with one gray-skinned, bony, talon-like hand.

Cutters Notch wasn't a large town despite being the county seat. I expected someone to drive down the road while we faced off. Yet, no one did. The houses to my left were too far off the road behind the trees to be of any help. The houses to my right were all dark. Pete's body and Ronnie's head were in my line of sight, behind the vampire now. My mind rushed to find a strategy, some action I could take to change the dynamic. Something. Anything. My only strategy was to delay, but dawn was still hours away.

I thought about trying to get in close. Pretend to let him have me, then stick the cook's blade into his ribs. Yet, my mind relived the moment Jerry Steinkamp shot the creature several times, point-blank in those same ribs—to no effect. What would a steel blade do that those lead bullets didn't? The bullets hurt him; his reaction made that apparent but hurt and kill were two different things. I needed to kill this monster.

Time was ticking but not nearly fast enough. The vampire was toying with me, indulging his curiosity for a little while. Eventually, he would make his move, and I would either die, or I would join him as one of his kind. I didn't want the first and completely rejected the second. I would die before I'd allow him to turn me.

Maurice continued his story. "I was made, as I will make you, in London when I was twenty-five years old—about the age you are now. Observe."

———•●•———

Suddenly, I was in a different place. I found myself standing on a cobblestone street. The streetlamps were actual flames inside glass bowls and sparsely placed. I was walking along a dark sidewalk alone, wearing uncomfortable shoes and an odd assortment of clothes. Buildings loomed on either side of the narrow streets. No moon lit up the starless, cloudy sky. Darkness lurked in every corner, draining away the streetlights into alleys and recessed doorways. Shadows spread like blackened cloaks across my path. A rat scurried around a wooden crate at the opening to an alley, disappearing as quickly as it appeared.

The person in whom I found myself paused at the alley. Through his eyes I could see a lighted window but not much else. Something clacked on the stones a few feet away. It sounded much like the clatter that the clawed toes of the vampire made as it danced for me.

In that moment, I realized where I was and in whom I was. Maurice was feeding his history into my mind.

"Who's there?" Maurice asked. There was no answer. After a moment, he asked again. "Who are you? What do you want? Why do you keep following me?" I felt the fear building within him. His hands were shaking.

Memories not my own rushed my mind. I'd been at a theatre with my parents—Maurice's parents—but I'd lost my temper. They were trying to control me, keeping me under their thumb, telling me whom to marry. I wanted my freedom, so I rushed off into the darkness. I needed space. Time to think.

"If you mean to rob me, you waste your time. I

have no coin," Maurice said, his voice cracking with fear.

There was no response at first, but two yellow orbs appeared, floating in the darkness. After a moment, they blinked.

Frightened, Maurice hurried away, looking back over his shoulder every few steps. His footfalls echoed off the stone walls of the two-story buildings. His heart was racing as he rushed along, pounding in his ears. He stopped at a doorway below a window through which a candle flickered. As he pounded, calling for help, the candle went dark.

"Help me, please," he called out toward the newly darkened window. No one responded. The few other windows that previously sported lights were now as dark as the streets below. He would find no refuge here.

Maurice spotted a pub at the next corner. *Surely someone will be there*, he thought. *Pubs are always open.* He crossed the street and sprinted past the next block of buildings, his shoes clacking on the cobblestones. Maurice grabbed the door, but it wouldn't budge, locked up tight. He squinted to read a sign attached to the door. It was difficult to make out, but it said something about closing before nightfall.

Behind him, steps click, click, clicked on the cobbles. Glancing over his shoulder, he spotted a dark-caped man approaching. He was tall, very tall. Too tall. Moving fast. As he watched, the man's left hand stretched out, and his nails scraped against the stone wall of a darkened home, trailing sparks as he moved along.

Maurice panicked and ran. Laughter echoed through the empty streets, bouncing from wall to wall and reverberating from the buildings ahead of him.

Desperate, he darted into an alley that opened just beyond the pub, hoping to cut over a street, hoping the next street would have more lights, more people. Someplace to go, someplace to get away. Boxes and crates were scattered in his path, causing him to bob and weave down the narrow corridor.

Halfway through, the alley abruptly ended. A wooden wall with hooks affixed across the top stood ahead, blocking his exit. He had no idea why. Like a mouse in a box trap, he had nowhere to run. His only option was to retrace his steps, but when he whipped around, the yellow orbs were staring at him from the spot where he'd entered the trap.

As I rode along within Maurice's memories, I felt his heart slamming inside his chest. I could sense his terror, a terror that I now shared.

The figure in the cape approached, slowly at first, then faster. The yellow eyes grew larger, more defined. Black pinpoint pupils emerged within the center of the glowing yellow irises.

There was a door to the right. Maurice didn't know where it led; he didn't care. He darted that way, frantically trying the handle. Locked. He pounded on the frame. "Help! Help me, please," he begged. No one responded. These were businesses, closed and locked until morning. Any occupants of the apartments above had learned to ignore disturbances in the night, locking themselves in for safety.

Terrified, Maurice turned back to the alley to find a dagger-toothed vampire standing before him. The monster wore a top hat which he then tipped toward him with a slight bow.

"I only seek a companion this evening," the creature explained with an accent I recognized as German. Then it laughed again. "And every evening after this one. Do not fear me. Instead of dying, you will be reborn. We will have adventures, you and I."

The last thing Maurice saw before my vision

ended was the widening of jaws and the darkness of the maw behind the teeth.

———•●•———

Back in Cutters Notch, Maurice raised his right hand and snapped his fingers. A streetlight went dark in the distance behind him. He snapped more, and as he did streetlamps continued to darken, starting with the furthest one. My heart raced faster and faster as the darkness approached. Soon, it was only he and I and the lamp towering between us.

"I can't be the companion you seek. I won't do it. I won't become what you became."

"Then you shall add to the carnage in the street. Your blood shall mingle with that of the others. Such a pity."

Midnight had come and gone. I could tell because I was losing my earliest active memories of entering Cutters Notch. The bloody death I'd envisioned had not been mine. It'd been Ronnie's murder. Apparently, mine was yet to come.

"What happened to your maker?" I asked. "You were his companion, were you not? I saw him within your memories."

"Frederick was immensely old. Even with me as his companion, he grew restless within our existence." Again, Maurice paused, perhaps drinking deeply from his thoughts, or perhaps just for effect. It was impossible to tell. "He sacrificed himself to the sun's rays in 1961."

I'm not sure how I managed to smile, but I did. "If you're so lonely, maybe you should follow his example," I suggested.

The vampire flew at me, fingers like claws, teeth bared, yellow eyes blazing. With no time to retrieve the knife, I braced for the blow and raised my hands as if to push the creature away. I don't know how, but at the point where the vampire was upon me, I pushed with my mind, and power surged, exiting my body. The blow caught Maurice in the chest and drove him back twenty yards. The same blow propelled my feet backward about an equal distance. Another newly discovered skill to take note of, assuming I survived.

"See? This is why I like you, young one." He laughed and flew at me again. The game was on.

Again, I shoved him back, and again, the effort propelled me in the opposite direction as more psychic energy left my mind. The rubber soles of my shoes skidded against the asphalt pavement of the roadway.

"You have astounding power for a human. I've never crossed paths with another like you. You *must* join me. Together, we could stop huddling in the darkness. We could rule. Conquer. Live like kings." Maurice giggled, giddy with delight. I, on the other hand, felt emboldened by my newly found power, yet terrified, horrified, and angry.

The vampire flew at me yet a third time. This time, I knocked him back even further, and my resulting position found me directly in front of Rose's driveway feeling drained. My mental gas tank was getting low. I couldn't keep this up. The next time or maybe the one after that, I wouldn't have the ability to keep him off me.

"You are strong," Maurice pointed out. Then, as if reading my mind, he added, "but your power is not endless. How long can you keep doing this? I, however, can do this all night. I'm like a prizefighter doing a little warm-up sparring." He danced around again, punching the air with curled-up talons for fists.

As I stood there watching him prance, I realized that I could see Rose's driveway—a very good sign. Maybe I wasn't as welcome as I originally had been before our magnificent kiss, but I wasn't banished either. The ghosts weren't blocking my mind. There it was—the gravel pathway angling back into the trees. Among the soaring oaks, I could see a welcoming porch light twinkling through the rustling leaves. After putting so much power into driving the vampire back, I didn't know if I could make it as far as her front door before collapsing in a heap in the underbrush. Still, maybe I didn't need to go that far.

When Maurice made his fourth attempt, instead of shoving him away, I sidestepped into the driveway, hoping against hope. I stopped in the same spot where Rose and I had watched Ronnie a few hours earlier— the place where the bully lost sight of us while we stood right in front of him. I poured the last wish I had into the hands of Rose's ghosts, that they would have the same effect on the vampire they had on everyone else.

Maurice skidded past and stumbled briefly before returning to my previous spot. "Nice move, Doc. Yet, you cannot lose me in the trees. I can see in the dark, and I can sense your presence wherever you go." The monster trotted to the right, then turned and trotted back, ending again in the last place I stood before ducking into the driveway. The breeze had picked up, so his cape was fluttering in the wind.

That last statement Maurice made was a lie, made so by the spectral power of about thirty ghosts. I stood right in front of him, and yet it was as if I were invisible. The yellow eyes drifted from side to side, up and down, but were unable to lock onto me. The creature cocked his head as if he were probing, seeking me with his mind. He was coming up empty. The vampire even flared his nostrils as he sniffed to catch my scent.

Maurice stepped up on the sidewalk. I stood a foot away. He couldn't smell me, but I could certainly smell him. Up close, he was rank with sickening sweetness. I suppose it was too much cologne covering up the fact that he never showered, and he walked around inside a body that wasn't truly alive but wouldn't rot.

The only thing between us was an unseen barrier generated by the ghosts in the house a quarter mile behind me. As the monster searched with its eyes and probed with its mind, I reached for the knife taped to my leg.

Apparently, the ghostly barrier also blocked sound because there was no reaction from Maurice when I pulled the duct tape off my skin, freeing the blade. After withdrawing the knife from my pants, I ran my finger carefully across the edge. It was very sharp.

"Where are you, Doc? I know you are near, but I sense nothing. How are you doing this?" He paused. "In fact, I sense absolutely nothing. No birds. No creatures of any type. Sometimes nothing is as helpful as everything. I feel every tiny mouse behind me and to either side, but nothing directly in front of me. You are somehow blocking me, but you cannot continue to evade me forever." Maurice extended his gray-skinned neck, turning his head to listen for my response.

It wasn't me blocking him, but I wasn't going to correct his error.

"Perhaps, I should walk toward that sense of nothingness. I might find you and whatever else you may be hiding inside. What do you think of that?"

I responded with a slashing steel blade. "That's a terrible idea!"

The knife's edge caught the vampire across the side of his throat, cutting cleanly into the skin, the tendons, the muscles, the arteries, and even the bone. I only had one shot, so I put everything into it—power I didn't know I had. One slash with all my might and Maurice's head joined Ronnie's as it rocked and rolled on Highway 257.

Seventeen

Journal Excerpts

The vampire once was an ordinary young man. His name was Maurice. Another older vampire turned him to make him his companion, the very thing he wanted from me.

We battled in the street. It seems I have the power to move things,

even monsters, with energy I push out of my mind.

That borrowed knife came in quite handy.

———•●•———

The vampire's body stayed erect for a while, staggering around, claws scratching at the air. When the head stopped rolling, Maurice's eyes continued to emit their yellow light, gazing out at the disconnected torso. I stepped from the trees with the monster's blood still dripping from the blade and poked the teetering torso. It lost its balance and fell over. The neck of the headless body aligned with its bodiless head a few feet away.

Satisfaction is a great feeling that is often missed in the aftermath of trauma. That wasn't the case for me. I felt tremendous satisfaction when Maurice's head left his body, and it amplified when I pushed said body to the pavement.

But it was short-lived.

In a moment that felt surreal, the head moved—on its own—through some previously unknown power of vampiric telekinesis. It slid neck first toward the body. The eyes glared at me. The mouth of sharp teeth moved up and down, but no sound came out.

"Oh, no you don't," I said, then kicked the head like a rubber ball to the other side of the street. Apparently, cutting off a vampire's head doesn't necessarily kill it. My work wasn't finished.

I wasn't sure what to do next. One of the pieces of lore I'd read in the library earlier said to put a wooden stake through the vampire's heart. That seemed a little fantastical, but what part of this whole crazy series of events wasn't fantastic? Another option would be to keep the two parts of Maurice's body sitting in the road—apart—until the sun came up and see what happened then. However, I had to believe the road would get busier as morning approached. At this point, most residents didn't know the extent of the carnage. Some would begin their workdays early only to be confronted with the blood and bodies strewn across the road.

The head moved again. Somehow, it was able to scoot itself across the pavement. Perhaps it was the same sort of mental energy I'd used to push Maurice back just a few moments ago. I needed to decide on a course of action to keep that ugly thing from reconnecting itself. My gut feeling was that Maurice was a tad more unhappy with me now, and probably no longer toyed with the idea of having me for his best friend.

Finally, headlights approached from the direction of Robbins Creek Road, coming up from behind the

General Store. The SUV sported a lightbar on the roof. I was still standing under a streetlight, clearly visible as it sped up, turned, and came to an abrupt stop twenty feet from my spot. Gator jumped from the driver's side. Calvin Churchill exited the passenger side.

"You okay, Doc?" Gator asked.

"I'm fine, but this guy's suffering a little separation anxiety." I pointed the knife at the still quivering torso on the pavement.

"I'll be dazzled!" Calvin spurted. "Doc, you got it." He almost danced in the street.

Gator spotted the head near the opposing curb. "How'd you manage it?"

I held up the large knife. It gleamed in the headlamps from the county vehicle. More of Maurice's vile blood dripped from the tip.

"We'll need to return this to the Quarry Pit, but Gator, it's not actually dead," I said. "Watch." I used the knife to point at Maurice's glowing face. As we studied it, the head moved again—about three inches in the direction of the body.

Following his own instructions to the other deputies, Gator withdrew his service weapon and shot Maurice square between the eyes. The bullet hole immediately resealed itself and disappeared. He shot it again. Same outcome.

"My God. How is that possible?" Gator took a couple of steps toward the head, then thought better of it. "What do we do?" He stared at me for a few seconds then shifted his gaze to Calvin. "Any ideas?"

Calvin shrugged.

Ignoring the vampire pieces on the roadway, I shifted the conversation. "Where've you guys been?" I was a little ticked off at these deputies who were supposed to protect and serve. Waving my arm toward the park, I added, "there are bodies strewn all the way to the other end of town. Ronnie's dead. Maurice here literally bit his head off and threw it at me. His two buddies from the scrapyard are dead, too, lying in the park. Pete, Ronnie's neighbor, has bled out into the gutter. And the librarian's corpse is lying headfirst down the steps of the library. Only that creature knows how many others he killed in your little town while you were AWOL. Blood is flowing down your main-street gutter like a little crimson river."

Calvin was silent, still staring at Maurice's head. Gator took a deep breath before responding. "We had our own run-in with this…this…whatever it is."

"Vampire."

"Right. Vampire. He attacked a little neighborhood up the road there. Specifically, the sheriff's house. He chased Rick's wife into her bedroom. She locked herself in and called us. Being the sheriff's wife, we all responded. It took us a while to search the house and the surrounding area, staying in pairs. After what happened to Jerry—"

"Rick's wife? Did he kill her, too?" No bedroom door would keep this creature out if he really wanted in. He would have had her before she even reached that room if he really wanted her.

"No. It rattled the door. Banged on it a few times. Threatened her. All while she was calling it in."

"A diversion," I said.

"What?" Calvin asked, pulling his attention back to our conversation.

"It was another diversion. Just like with those girls coming out of the garage earlier. He wanted you to look in the wrong place while he did his work somewhere else. The vampire got you out of the way so he could do his nasty business in town. If he'd wanted to kill her, he would have. Is Anders still with his wife?"

"Yeah," Gator answered, "and, frankly, he's

messed up. He's blaming himself for Jerry."

"How's Judy?"

"Shaken up. We drove her home before all hell broke loose at Rick's house."

The head scooted another four inches. I shoved it back to the curb with my toe, being careful to avoid the mouthful of teeth that were chomping wordlessly. Then, I turned to go to the dumpster next to the General Store.

"Where're you going?" Gator grabbed my elbow.

"I'm going to see if I can find a plastic bag or something. We need to contain that head so it can't reattach itself to the body. I assume that's what it wants to do, right?"

"What about your backpack?" Calvin asked.

"That's an idea, but I seem to keep my whole life in there. I don't want to get vampire blood all over the inside."

As we all peered at the bodiless head, it was Gator who came up with a bright idea. "I have something in the back of my unit. Hang on." He strode to the rear of his Ford and opened the tailgate. A few seconds later, he returned with a bowling-ball bag. "This should do the trick. I just bought it at a flea market, but I don't really need it."

The three of us gathered around the head. The thing's lips moved over the dagger-like teeth as if Maurice was trying to talk to us.

"His name was Maurice," I shared. "A very long time ago, he was just a man like any one of us." Maurice glared up at us with his unblinking yellow eyes. They still glowed brightly in the darkness. He was still in there; I saw a little sadness in those soulless windows. I marveled that the creature still carried the ability to be sad. "He was tracked down, cornered, and turned into the monster you see by another even older vampire."

Gator knelt and pulled the mouth of the bag wide

open. "Cal, drop that thing in."

"How? It ain't got no hair, and with those teeth snapping like that, I'll be snarkled if I know how to do it."

I pointed at the ears. "You get one and I'll grab the other. We'll drop the head in together."

Calvin stood to one side, while I moved into position. Just as we were about to pick it up, the head suddenly skittered away—fast—toward the body still quivering on the other side of the road. Maurice was making a last-ditch effort to escape.

"What the hell?" Gator exclaimed as the head sped past him.

"Get it!" I screamed. "Don't let it reach the body. If it reattaches, we'll all be screwed."

Gator leapt at the vampire's head like he was diving for home plate, bowling-ball bag in hand, and slapped the open leather container over Maurice's face just inches before it found purchase on the torso. He yanked it up, zipped it closed, and locked in the vampire's fate. We thought so at the time, anyway.

"Now what?" I asked. "Do we bury the pieces in two different places? How do we keep these two parts permanently separated?" Maybe the head was like a battery that would eventually run down without the power supply of the torso to keep it charged.

Calvin had fallen completely silent. No more colorful words. As I rambled on about how to keep the vampire helpless, he wandered over to examine the torso, leaving Gator and me to work out a plan.

"Let's toss the head and the body in the back of the Explorer," Gator eventually said as he looked toward the west on Highway 257. "I have an idea."

Pulling Calvin from his thoughts, Gator coerced him into grabbing an arm. Gator grabbed the other, and I snagged the feet. Together, we hoisted the heavy body into the cargo hold of the Ford. We rested the head-bag between the monster's feet. I double-checked to make sure the bowling-ball bag was securely closed.

Gator radioed in the rest of the mess in town to the balance of the small force of deputies while Calvin took shotgun, and I crawled in the backseat. "The vampire's dead, but we've got bodies along 257—the library, the park, Pete Smith's house. You can't miss it."

He didn't use code; he just laid it out for all ears to hear. If someone was monitoring a police scanner somewhere, they got a shock, I'm sure.

— • ● • —

Ten minutes and one cut padlock later, the three of us were standing in front of the car crusher inside Bill Castle's scrapyard. The moon was shining brightly in the night sky and reflecting off the twisted metal all around us. The tires that previously hid Jasper Fresno were piled here and there. The truck was gone leaving a large gap to the left of the crusher. Jasper was nowhere to be seen; apparently, he'd moved on, giving me yet another taste of satisfaction.

"You know how to run this thing?" I asked Gator.

"Yeah. It's been years, though. After my baseball career didn't pan out and my foray into homelessness, I worked here for a little while. Then I moved on to become the huge success in law enforcement that I am now." He chuckled before continuing. "It's simple, really. Power it up. There's a couple buttons—up and down. Then, abracadabra, you've got a flat-metal disc instead of an Oldsmobile."

The car crusher consisted of two huge, thick, flat-steel plates. The base was stationary, and hydraulic cylinders drove down the top plate. When a scrap vehicle was placed between the steel slabs, and the pressure was activated, the top plate compressed the car or truck with tremendous power into a twisted metal pancake. There was already one smashed car left unattended in the machine—an old Cutlass Supreme. An oversized forklift sat with its forks up against the side of the Cutlass.

While Gator and I stood there perusing the technology that was part of the junk-car industry, Calvin wandered to the rear of the Ford Explorer, opened the rear hatch, and peered in at what remained of Maurice the vampire. From the corner of my eye, I saw him open the bag containing the head and stare inside. He hadn't had much to say since we loaded the monster pieces in the truck. I chalked it up to the overwhelming, fantastical nature of the whole series of events.

"So, what's the plan here, Gator?" I asked. "Do we need to pull that car out of the way?"

"Nope. We'll back the fork truck up so we can get at it. Then, we'll place the head on one end of the smashed car and the torso on the other. After that, it's just a matter of activating the hydraulics to obliterate that creature and smash it into vampire juice."

Gator jumped into the seat of the forklift. Apparently, they weren't worried about theft because the keys were still in the ignition. He started it, backed it up, and left it idling as he jumped back down to rejoin me.

Behind us, something thumped. Gator heard it, too. We turned together to see an ungodly sight. Calvin stood unblinking in the moonlight with Maurice's headless body leaning neck upward against his legs. In his hands, he held the vampire's head by the ears, glowing eyes, gleaming teeth, and all.

"What the hell are you doing?" I exclaimed. "Don't let them touch!"

Out of Calvin's mouth came Maurice's European accent. "I think I'll not let you crush me, my good fellows. I have other plans for this night. There is more fun to be had at your expense."

Before we could react, Calvin lowered Maurice's head to line up with the gaping neck on his torso. As soon as they touched, a bright red line formed at the connection, and the flesh reattached. The monster immediately stood to his full height, throwing Calvin aside like a used towel. Maurice twisted his head back and forth, testing the bond, then rubbed it with his right hand. "Ah, right as rain once again. It is not the first time someone has attempted to behead me." The vampire smiled a toothy grin. "Vampires. We're a tricky lot, are we not?"

Gator pulled his weapon and shoved me aside as he took aim.

"We had his head cut off," I said, "and he didn't die. You already shot him in the forehead—twice—and he didn't die. I don't think that gun will hurt him much now." I'd left my knife in Gator's unit. Besides, I'd lost the element of surprise. I began to search for something, anything I could use for a weapon. There was lots of twisted metal but nothing useful within easy reach.

Maurice approached slowly, hands spread out and hung low, palms up with his fingers curled in like claws. We backed away until we were up against the Olds Cutlass with nowhere else to go. Calvin was unmoving, lying still on the dirt, twenty yards away.

"Doc," Maurice said, "I have come to the unavoidable conclusion that I have misjudged you. You simply will not make a good companion. Perhaps the taste of your blood on my tongue will satisfy my fury…perhaps not."

Gator fired nine times. A skilled marksman, he hit Maurice nine times in a tight pattern in the center of the creature's chest. Blood oozed from the wounds, further staining the vampire's ruffled white shirt, but otherwise the bullets had no effect.

Maurice took his time. One step. Two steps. He knew we had nowhere to run. We were like mice trapped in a box with a cat. He was the cat wanting to play with his grinning teeth and glowing eyes.

I tried to shove the vampire away with another mental blow, but I felt it slam back to me, parried by the monster's mind. "I am on to your powers, young one. No more telekinetic games. We are reaching the end of our acquaintance."

The vampire lurched, feigning an all-out attack. We flinched. Maurice laughed. Despite his words, it was all still a game to him. "Doc, I believe I will kill you last. You will see all your companions die before I take you. Then, like those girls I released earlier, I will drain you slowly, over time. Little sips when I get thirsty, larger sips when I'm hungry. I wonder how long you will last. Perhaps a week? Not more than two. All the while, you'll be reliving the loss of all your friends."

"Not likely," I replied. "I won't give them another thought after day one."

"We shall see," Maurice said with a grin. "Oh, we shall see."

Something changed in the vampire's demeanor. It was subtle, but it told us the games really were at an end. Maurice's gaze turned from yellow to red. He raised his hands and began to move in with purpose, jaws wide, teeth bared.

Gator was out of bullets in his clip, but he still had his Taser. He pulled the yellow plastic device from his belt and fired. "Run!" he screamed at me. The prongs hit Maurice in the chest. The electricity jolted the monster, and the vampire jerked back, shaking violently, halting his progress.

Then, the forklift behind Maurice surged to life. It wasn't Calvin as he was still sprawled in the dirt, apparently unconscious.

"You killed my son," Bill Castle roared from the driver's seat. "You evil bastard, son of-a-hell hound!" He gunned the industrial truck's engine and drove one of the forks hard into the vampire's back, impaling him with its sharpened edge. Then, he lifted the forks, pulling the monster off his feet. Maurice hung there, feet dangling and arms swinging, still stunned from the Taser.

The prongs were imbedded in the vampire's chest, and Gator still held the weapon in his hand. He gave the monster another jolt causing Maurice to cry out in pain. I saw surprise in the monster's eyes, and something else—fear.

"Get outta the way," Bill ordered. "I'm gonna end this thing right here, right now."

After pushing the vampire into the machine over the top of the ancient Oldsmobile, pinning him against the back wall, Bill jumped down and hit the button to activate the hydraulics on the crusher. Slowly, the top jaw descended, first closing the gap, then compressing the monster's body. After the car crusher had a firm grip, Bill backed out the forks, leaving the vampire inside.

Maurice screamed, but there was no escape. The press of the crusher's jaw smashed the monster flat, pulverizing bone and pushing out all fluids until he was nothing more than a flat, oblong disc of a bad memory.

Bill leapt from the fork truck and joined Gator and me as we looked on. "Let's leave it smashed in there like that until dawn," he said. "Then we can see what the sun does to what's left of it."

Being mid-June, the nights were short. Still, dawn was a few hours away when Bill Castle crushed the vampire. While we waited in anxious anticipation for those bright morning rays, the Bowen County Sheriff's Department did a great deal of work. First, Gator called the sheriff. He joined us at the scrapyard ten minutes later, relieved that his wife was safe.

They took Bill Castle into custody. He'd been listening in on a police scanner when Gator had radioed in the carnage in Cutters Notch. Rushing out, he found Ronnie's body in the park, followed by his head near the boy's home. His anger as a father carried him in pursuit of Maurice until he arrived just in time to rescue us.

He may have saved our lives, but he still killed Jasper Fresno and hid his body under a pile of tires for thirty years. He was a hero, but a hero with a past for which a debt was due.

The other deputies, free from their duty searching the woods around the sheriff's house, returned to town to find the bloody carnage. To their credit, they swallowed the trauma and worked diligently to collect the remains of their neighbors and process the scenes. By the time the sun rose, most of the worst of it had been cleaned up.

Judy Steinkamp, her loss fresh and her grief barely contained, also joined our vigil waiting for the sunrise. I met her as she exited her car. We stood face-to-face. After a moment, I leaned forward, and she met me, pressing our foreheads together. I wrapped my arms around her and held her as she wept. "He was such a good son," she sobbed.

It seemed the night would never end, that the stars

would never recede into the sky. Then, all at once, as if there existed some sort of natural alarm clock, the birds began to sing. They were all around, even in hidden nests within the piles of junked cars. Their songs spoke of the imminent bloom of hope coming from the eastern sky.

There it was. The glow, the orange-pink brightness just before the sun slipped above the horizon. Watching the illumination grow across the land filled my soul with joy. We'd made it. Not all of us, but most of us. Gator and Calvin were alive. Sheriff Anders was still here. The little town of Cutters Notch would suffer from deep loss, but it would go on.

My thoughts drifted to Rose, that beautiful flower. Her image caused my heart to yearn for her. For her touch. For her kiss. For what could be and what might be. At the same time, I was sad because my first memories of her would disappear from my mind in a couple more hours.

As I daydreamed of soft lips and warm embraces, the sun broke fully into the new day. The sound of the hydraulics being reactivated on the car crusher yanked me back to reality. The jaw, with the bright light of dawn shining directly upon it, slowly began to rise.

The gap opened between the Olds Cutlass and the solid-steel plate. The sun slipped inside. The blood and the flattened flesh of the vampire began to sizzle as the light progressed. In moments, the mechanical jaw was fully retracted, the sun was in its full glory, and the body of the vampire disappeared into a hot mist that evaporated as it rose.

Maurice was now free to play his music in the sun. He would never again hurt anyone.

Eighteen
Journal Excerpts

Vampires are very hard to kill. I suppose being undead

makes them hard to make fully dead. Still, we got him there. Maurice is gone.

Cutters Notch suffered some terrible losses, but they will go on.

Some fantastic people live in this strange little town—

people I've grown fond of having in my life. I'm going to miss them.

Especially Rose. I wish I could stay, but my instinct is drawing me away.

I'm compelled to keep walking, take in the journey, and eventually reach my destination in Florida. Who knows? Maybe I'll come back someday.

———— • ● • ————

You've long since figured out that I survived. The new day dawned, and as it progressed, the memories of my one adventurous day in Cutters Notch began to slip from my mind. In another few hours, I would no longer recall anything about Jasper

Fresno, Ronnie Castle, or Maurice the Vampire. All the trauma and loss of the night of terror would fade away as my mind created a clean slate on which to experience new things.

Before leaving town, I stood on the sidewalk directly across from the General Store, my backpack loaded up with water bottles and snacks provided by my friends at the Sheriff's Office. Along with those necessities, they'd also supplied me with a change of clothes. Now, I had something to change into when I found some way to wash what I'd been wearing.

A large flatbed truck rolled past me before turning onto Bluff Road, headed uphill. Diesel fumes poisoned the air as it went by. I had a good idea where it was going, and I knew its trip was in vain. No load was available for pick up this morning at the mansion above the cliff.

It was about 9 a.m., and Rose was inside the store. I could see her through the plate-glass window. She was behind the counter taking care of a customer, her long wavy hair draping her shoulders and her smile brightening the new day.

I wanted to march across the road, pull open the doors of the little store, and take her in my arms in front of all of Cutters Notch—the age difference be damned. I wanted to be hers and for her to be mine. My tears flowed as I stood there yearning for what could never be. She needed to break the ghosts' hold on her, something I sensed I couldn't help with, and I was being pulled toward Florida with other adventures along the way. I couldn't linger, as much as my heart wanted to stay around.

As if to prove the point, I could no longer remember where she lived. I thought it was somewhere close, but it just wouldn't come to me. It was too soon to be my memory issue, so that's how I knew that my welcome had been revoked. The ghosts that held her and protected her didn't want me to come back. They'd come to my rescue when I needed them, but that need had passed.

It was time to move on, yearning or no yearning. Behind me was the road to the bluff. To my right and left rolled Highway 257. In front of me was Robbins Creek Road. All viable choices for a wanderer with no specific place to be at day's end. I glanced at my journal, and it reminded me that Sarasota, Florida was my ultimate destination. Sarasota was south. Robbins Creek Road headed south. It seemed as good a choice as any.

I took one more long look at Rose. Again, the yearning burned in my heart. Ignoring its pleading, I passed by the window, forcing my eyes to focus further down the road until she was out of sight.

A quarter mile south, I crossed an old steel-grated bridge over what I supposed was Robbins Creek. A few more steps and I passed a large white farmhouse sitting at the mouth of a cul-de-sac. The short street was lined with small ranch-style houses. An empty basketball court was at the entrance. Weeds were growing through cracks in the playing surface. It seemed like a common little neighborhood where nothing of note ever happened and I kept walking.

The forest rose and fell as I passed through. Old farms came and went. The road wound east, then west, then south again. Eventually, it spilled out onto a larger road. With each passing step, more memories faded until late that night, my precious memory of kissing Rose slipped away from me. I curled up on the floor of someone's shed as the rain pitter-pattered the metal roof, savoring my last glimpses of her reddish-brown hair. I had to read the notes in my journal to remember why she felt special to me.

Somewhere in the night, Maurice's teeth, yellow

eyes, and his terrifying actions were wiped from my mind as well. The vampire's horror now only existed as words on my notebook's pages.

I slipped out of the shed with the sun already high in the morning sky. The residents had left earlier, and the nearby home appeared empty, so I took a chance and refilled my bottles with water from a spigot sticking through the home's foundation. As I closed the valve, the last flash of a beautiful woman behind a store window evaporated from my memories. Rose was gone.

My slate was clean, ready for more memories to be made and lost. More mysteries to solve, then forget. Maybe more monsters to vanquish.

Epilogue
Journal Excerpt
I met the girl of my dreams today.
She's the most beautiful girl I've ever met.
Her name is Kelly Sue.

* ● * ─

Over the next several days, my notes say that I walked south and east across Southern Indiana, meandering through small towns, skirting larger ones. I slept on the back porches and inside the various outbuildings of unknowing homeowners. One night, I joined some homeless folks under a bridge north of the Ohio River near Louisville, Kentucky. Another rainy night, I slept inside a concrete culvert atop a stack of similar pipes, just to keep dry.

Nothing of note happened except that I began to dream of what I thought was a vicious dog. It would growl and snarl and snap at me, jarring me awake. Each day, I'd soon forget it like so many other dreams, but I did note it in the journal. After three days, I saw the pattern. A dream on repeat in my world apparently meant something, so I began to follow my directional instinct with more purpose.

On June thirtieth at ten in the morning, I stood at

the pinnacle of the Ohio River bridge leading from Madison, Indiana to Milton, Kentucky, enjoying the view upriver. The sky was blue with large puffs of white clouds drifting across, occasionally blocking the sun. The bridge itself was busy with traffic, cars and trucks traversing in both directions, but I paused along the pedestrian walkway, leaning on the steel railing.

Below, a tugboat was pushing two large, flat barges filled with coal downriver to feed the power plants that kept this part of the world energized. A man waved up at me. I waved back.

A speedboat sped along, headed upriver—two couples out for a day on the water in swim trunks and bikinis. "Woo-hoo," screamed the women as they waved at me, beverages in hand. The men only glared. I waved at all of them.

The vision of teeth and blood hit me without warning. One moment, I was watching ducks paddle around a large rock and the next, I was standing in a darkened town square, looking out from another person's eyes. A large stone structure loomed above me. At the sight of a sign on the door—Carroll County Courthouse—my host turned a circle, taking in the surroundings—a useful move because having a vision didn't help if I didn't know where I was. With my back to the government building, I could see lights bobbing up and down, moving slowly from right to left between and behind some low-set, old buildings across the street. I heard water flowing. An engine churning. The river was down there.

It appeared to be late at night and I heard movement nearby. Snarling, growling. My host investigated. As he rounded a corner, he found an oversized, half-upright canine as it ripped open the abdomen of an old man. The man's eyes stared at me, blankly, empty, dead. The canine, meanwhile, was oblivious to my observation as it snarled and tore and slurped up the blood.

The murderous beast was huge, the largest dog I'd ever seen. Of course, the only ones I could remember were in front yards or on leashes as I trekked across the countryside and through the town of Madison over the previous twenty-four hours. Maybe I'd seen larger ones and simply didn't recall them. On the other hand, maybe this was a wolf. It seemed like a strange place for a wolf, but what did I know?

The belltower of the courthouse standing in the middle of the square tolled twelve times—midnight. I didn't know if this was a vision of something that had already happened, or something yet to happen. Since my premonitions tended to happen within twenty-four hours, and the clock had tolled midnight, I may only have fourteen hours or so to save that man's life. However, since I was seeing through another person's eyes, it seemed likely to have already occurred, but I had no idea how long ago. Either way, I needed to investigate. More accurately, I was driven to investigate. I could do nothing else. It was a compulsion.

The monster finished ripping at the dead man's flesh. Blood dripped from its jaws and soaked its maw. Its eyes glowed red as it sniffed at the night air. Light from a nearly full moon illuminated the creature as it stood on its hind legs to howl—such an eerie, mournful sound.

The moonbeams revealed a surprising sight. The huge canine wore blue jeans.

Without warning, the monster charged me, leaping at my throat, teeth bared. My host threw up his hands; he screamed and jerked away.

I awoke from the daytime nightmare and found myself still on the bridge over the Ohio River in the middle of the day. My feet were sprawled out in front of me; my back rested against a large I-beam. My clothes were drenched in sweat. Behind me, tires squealed, and a car stopped. Horns honked. I had a lump on the back of my head, and it hurt something awful.

"Are you okay? Are you hurt? What happened?"

The most beautiful girl I'd ever seen stepped over the berm onto the walkway near me. She stood haloed by the sunlight, a blond angel. With her golden locks blowing in the wind, she knelt beside me, repeating her urgent questions.

"I'm okay," I answered as I took in the bright blue of her eyes. She wore sandals; her toes stuck out with pink polish on the nails. Her brown legs were a million miles long as they sprang from her cutoff khaki shorts. Her tanned arms flowed from a simple white, button-down blouse with short sleeves. A colorful, flowery tattoo extended down her arm from beneath the fringe of her shirt.

The beauty looked to be in her early twenties with smooth skin and concerned eyes. She had multiple earrings, rings on her fingers, a gold loop hung from her exposed belly button, and she even had a ring on one of her little toes.

"I saw you fall. You were standing at the railing. Then you just fell back hard and slammed into the support post there. Are you sure you're okay? Did you hit your head?"

Her stopped car was blocking traffic, and horns blared as traffic backed up behind her. She waved them off, glaring. "Give me a minute to check on him, all right?"

"I'm fine," I said as I scrambled to my feet. "My mind was somewhere else, I guess. I must have gotten dizzy and fell over. No big deal."

"Can I give you a ride somewhere?" She smiled,

concern in her eyes. "Where were you headed?"

I thought back to my vision. The courthouse had a sign. "Um, I need to go to the Carroll County Courthouse." The vision of the canine's teeth still hung right under the surface within my mind's eye.

"Perfect. I'm headed to Carrollton myself. We keep a boat at the marina on the other side of town. Jump in." She pointed past me to her waiting car.

"Are you sure? You don't even know me."

"I'm a good judge of character, and I can tell you've got it."

"Got what?"

"Character."

"How can you tell?"

"Does it matter? Like I said friend, jump in."

Stopped pickups, box trucks, and various cars waited impatiently. A man hung out of his driver's side window and screamed. Expletives I guessed, although I couldn't hear them over the engine noise. His hand gestures and the look on his face translated the message.

"If you're sure then."

"I am. Let's get going before Jim Bob over there gets out to make his point." She smiled so sweetly that I couldn't imagine anyone being angry at her.

I rounded her classic black Pontiac Trans Am with a giant eagle on the hood and climbed into the passenger seat. The interior with tanned leather seats was impeccable—clean and in pristine condition. "What's your name?" I asked her.

"Kelly Sue Walker. And yours?"

"Some people call me Doc, but I'm pretty sure I'm not a doctor. It's just a nickname."

"Welcome to Kentucky, Doc," she said as she dropped the shifter into drive, gunned the engine, and popped the clutch. She left rubber on the roadway as the big engine drove the muscle car to the far end of the long bridge.

I'm not sure where it came from or why, but I looked at her with just one more question: "Are you actually the age you are?"

She didn't respond, but Kelly Sue gave me a sly smile, winked, and drove me to my next adventure.

Michael DeCamp is a multi-genre author of both fantasy thrillers and spiritual enrichment books. Married with two grown daughters, he is a native of Muncie, Indiana, and currently resides in Indianapolis. He enjoys history, reading thrilling stories, podcasting, great movies, and active vacations. Keep updated on his books and other projects by visiting his website and registering for his occasional newsletter. www.authormichaeldecamp.com

Author Contact Information

Mailing Address
Michael DeCamp
P.O. Box 39056
Indianapolis, IN 46239
Website
www.authormichaeldecamp.com
Email
michael@authormichaeldecamp.com
Facebook
@authormichaeldecamp
Instagram
@mdecamp1985
Amazon Profile
www.amazon.com/author/michaeldecamp

Other Books by Michael DeCamp

The Cutters Notch Trilogy & Related Stories
Abandon Hope: A Cutters Notch Novel – Book One
Nozomi's Battle: A Cutters Notch Novel – Book Two
Cutters Notch Interludes: A Collection of Short Stories

Reckless Abandon: A Cutters Notch Novel – Book Three

<u>Non-Fiction/Spiritual Enrichment</u>

Loving Out Loud: Learning to Love in a Hate-Filled World

Loving Out Loud Companion Workbook